I0588058

I LOVE YOU

A Novel

Billie Dureya Shell

I LOVE YOU

Copyright © 2021

All rights reserved to Billie Dureyea Shell.

No part of this publication may be reproduced, distributed or transmitted in any form or by any means, including photocopying, or other electronic or mechanical methods, without the prior written permission of the publisher, except in the case of brief quotations embodied in critical reviews and certain noncommercial uses permitted by copyright law.
Any references to historical events, real people or real places are used factiously. Names, characters, and places are products of the authors imagination.

Front Cover Image By graphic designer Billie Dureyea Shell & Kenny Writes

First Printing Edition 2021

ISBN 9781735023489

This book is dedicated to:

My Uncle Woody Only Duarther and My Little Cousin
Quincella I Love You
Let's Make This Juice Business Blow up

ACKNOWLEDGEMENT

First and foremost I have to give honor to My Lord And Saviour Jesus Christ without him now of this would be possible. 2020 was a MUTHA FUCCA Corona Virus made shit hard 4 niggas but we made it threw y'all keep your head up and know that God got us, no matter they throw in our way no one can stop what God has plan for you...

Its 2021 now FUCC 2020 and Covid 19.... Now to my family momma I love you and you no I got you no matter what. You mean the world 2 me oh and NO MORE PINCHING LOL. To my little sister Glenda I love you blackie, you No I Got You always

To my Wife Shatoya Shell you get on my damn nerves 💀 but I wouldnt trade you 4 anything In the world I love 🖤 you more then words can ever express. To all my children 👶👶 I love y'all Jazmine, Ant'Tuan, Davon, Anthony, David, Lil Dureyea, Alura, Queen Diavion, Cameron, Preniece, Shaniece and Tajh I love u all and I'll 4ever have ur back you all give me a reason 2 smile... to my cousin Zane RIP nigga I miss u more then anyone will ever no, your always remembered love you bro. to my cousin Ty I miss you thank 4 looking out 4 me and Zane you played a big part in my life and I always looked up to you I love you... Uncle Woody I miss you and love you, you no your my favorite uncle... To my nigga Jamal love you, my brothers Lawrence and fred thank 4 showing me the game I love yall 4 that. To my oldest sister Nedra love you thank you 4 always having my back. to my family uncles anties cousins etc.. I love y'all even those of you that act funny as fuck

To my dark side niggas y'all no what it is YAAH GANG....
Now to all my readers and fans I love you thanks for reading I
hope u enjoy this book as much as I enjoy writing
them with this Corona Virus 19 shit there ain't shit to do but
write so I'm on my shit with that being said y'all be safe cover
your face and love each other life is short so love the ones that
really love I'm gone no. enjoy the book

STAY SAFE

Author Billie Dureyea Shell

THERE'S NOTHING U CANNOT DO
IF U PUT UR MIND 2 IT.

All you nigga's got EDD money so aint no excuse
why you can't get a book LOL

PROLOGUE

Mya opened up her eyes and wondered where she was. Looking left and right, she noticed that nothing looked familiar. When she tried to move, she felt a sharp pain in her hand. Lifting her hand, she saw that she had an IV attached. "Where am I?" Mya thought to herself as she focused her eyes and looked around. She started to panic and as soon as she was about to attempt to get out of the bed, a nurse walked in. "Ms. Adams, I see you woke up." The nurse said walking over to Mya. "Where am I?" Mya asked still confused, and with her vision a little cloudy. "You are at Ft. Washington Hospital Center." "What am I doing at the hospital?" She asked, looking at the nurse quizzically. "You were brought here badly beaten and close to death." The nurse said informing Mya of her condition upon arrival. She laid her head back on the pillow, lost in her own thoughts when something occurred to her. She reached down and touched her still rounded stomach. The nurse read her mind and said "You delivered a baby girl." "Is she ok?" Mya asked. "She is doing fine." The nurse assured Mya. "Can I see her?" "How about I bring her to you after you talk to the doctor?" The nurse said. "Ok, thank you." Mya said relaxing in the bed. When the nurse left, Mya began to think about her life. She was 22 and went through more stuff than a woman in her lifetime. Taking a deep breath she looked up at the ceiling and began to think about when her life got so fucked up.

Chapter 1

IN THE BEGINNING 1987...

———◦·❯❯❮◦⧫◦❯❯❮◦·———

It was a cold winter day in December 1987. Liz was 8 months pregnant at home cleaning and cooking dinner for her husband Michael Adams and their two kids. Without the knowledge of knowing where her husband was at, she never slacked on her wifely duties. Michael Adams was one of the most powerful drug dealers in the DC area in the 80's. On the street he was known as Big Mike. He stood 6'5 with a slim frame, smooth chocolate skin, with deep waves in his hair, and a full beard. Big Mike was known to be a smooth talker to the ladies, and trigger happy to anybody that disrespected him. He met Liz when she was 16 years old and knew the sassy Spanish girl was going to be his. Liz was 5'4 and so beautiful. She had long dark hair and hips that all the men wanted to hold, with full lips and brown eyes that would draw you in when you look in them. Liz liked Big Mike but she knew he was 20 years old. She fell head over hills for Big Mike not caring about the age difference. When she started to spend more time with him, her parents put her out and she moved in with him. As soon as she moved in with Mike, she got pregnant with their son Mike Jr. Liz stopped going to school shortly after having her son and became a full time mom and wife to Mike. Two years after having Mike Jr., Liz had another baby. This time she had a girl named Laurel. She was happy with her life but felt empty. Mike was never there, she had to raise two children by herself, and when he did come home he would yell, or beat on her. She wanted to escape Mike, but didn't know who or where to go. As soon as Liz turned 20, Mike took her and the children to the courthouse so they could get married legally. After getting married and Liz had taken his last name Adams, she thought things were going to change but they didn't. Mike kept going out cheating, leaving her and the children alone. On a cold December night, Liz cooked dinner, cleaned the house, put her children to bed and sat on the couch waiting for her husband to come in. In the process of waiting, she felt a sharp pain in her side. Next thing she knew her water broke. Having two children already, she was prepared and knew what to do. She picked up her phone and called Mike's car phone but received no answer. She tried again and this time he answered. "What woman! I'll be home soon." Mike said through the phone while the young girl in his car gave him head. "Papi my water broke." Liz said. "What? You not due till January" Mike said pushing the young girls head more into his lap. "I know, but she is coming now." Liz said frantically. "Shit, I'm on my way." Mike said hanging up and letting the young girl finish giving him head. Liz went upstairs showered, packed the bag, and called the doctor. When she finished everything, Mike still wasn't there so she called a cab. After she called a cab, she called one of her friends to stay with the children since they were still sleep. Liz rode to the hospital by herself, no husband to support her along the way. Mike pulled up at the house and rushed in looking for Liz. "Baby" Mike yelled. "She left." Liz's friend said who didn't like Mike. "Where she did go, and how did she get there?" Mike asked mugging her. "She took a cab. She got tired of waiting for your sorry ass." She said rolling her eyes at him. Mike couldn't stand the sight of Liz's friend let alone any of her friends. Leaving out the house, he jumped in his car and rushed to Los Angeles General where he knew she would be. Arriving at the hospital, he asked around until they gave him directions to Liz. As soon as he got in the room, they were preparing her for a C-section. "Baby what's going on?" Mike asked getting nervous. "The baby's cord is wrapped around her neck and I lost a lot of blood so we press for time." Liz said through her oxygen mask. Mike went with her and held her hand the whole time during the C-section. After the doctor unwrapped the cord from the baby's neck, they proudly held up a healthy baby girl. Mike held his daughter and let a tear fall. He knew if she hadn't made it, it was his fault for taking too long. "What is her name?" the nurse asked smiling at the sight of father and daughter together. "Mya Faith Adams." Mike said looking at the baby. December 15, 1987 Mya was born and that was the start of her crazy life.

Chapter 2

1997

Liz was sitting at the table helping Mya and Laurel with their homework, while Mike Jr. played outside, when Big Mike walked in the house. He was home earlier than he normally would be home, so Liz didn't have dinner ready for him. Big Mike walked in the kitchen where he saw that all three of his women were sitting at the table. He gave Laurel and Mya a kiss on the forehead, but when he got to Liz he said "Where dinner at?" "It's not done yet. You home earlier than normal. So..." Liz began to say. Before she knew it, Big Mike slapped her so hard she fell out of her chair. Liz touched her lip and saw the blood on her fingertips. Scared to move, Liz laid on the floor as Big Mike beat her over and over in front of his daughters. Laurel and Mya cried as they watched their mother get beaten. When Big Mike finally got tired, he stopped and just looked down at a bleeding and swollen faced Liz. "Get your ass up and fix me some dinner. Shit betta not take long either." Big Mike said walking out of the kitchen, leaving her and the girls there. Liz got up weakly and did as she was told. She was too embarrassed to look at her daughters, so she just focused on making dinner. Laurel and Mya were always scared when their father came home because he would always beat on Liz in front of them. Even though he never raised a hand to them, they didn't want him to ever turn his rage on them. Mya loved her father a lot and was a daddy's girl, but when he beat on her mother she wanted him dead. She never understood how her mother just took the beatings and say she loved him after. Laurel on the other hand hated Mike's guts. She promised when she got older and if he was still beating on her mother, she would kill him. Mike Jr. repeatedly asked his mother to leave his dad, but she always told him she couldn't because she loved him. .... It was a normal night in the Adams household after the incident. After dinner, everything cooled down and Big Mike left and went back on the block. At 3AM the house phone rung, waking Liz. "Hello" Liz said sleepily. "You have a collect call from "Mike"" the recording said. Liz pushed one and picked up fast. "Baby is you ok?" Liz asked. "Naw, babe I got knocked. They got me on some bullshit. I should be out tomorrow." Mike said like it was nothing. "Do you need anything? You want me to do anything?" Liz asked feeling sorry for her husband. Even though he just beat her less than 12 hours ago, she couldn't help but worry about him. "All I need you to do is stay by the phone. I'm going to call some people." "Ok. I love you." Liz said softly. "Yeah, this will prove if you really love me." Mike said hanging up. Liz felt a little relieved that Mike was in jail. On the other hand she only been with him and he took care of her. She didn't know what to expect from this situation. The next morning, Mike was called to court. Liz was right at the court to show her support for her man. He was being charged with drug possession and a gun that was dirty. On top of that, he also got charged with two murders that happened in the early 80's. Mike was sentenced to 30 years in federal prison. All he could think about was his family and how they were going to survive. Mike told her about the stashed money he had saved for her and the kids, but he knew it wasn't going to last for 30 years. After Mike went to prison, Mya took it hard, where as Laurel was happy and Mike Jr. didn't really care what happened to his father.

Chapter 3

THE YEAR 2000

It had been 3 years since Mike went to jail and the money he left for his family was gone. Mike didn't even leave his family enough to survive longer than a year on. They had to down grade from their house and move to the projects of S.E. Washington, D.C. They went from a four bed room house to a two bedroom apartment. Liz had to get a job to support her family and to put food on the table. The food stamps the government gave her were barely enough to get 2 weeks' worth of groceries. To have 3 growing kids in the house, she knew food would go fast. Mya was now a 12 going on 25 year old in middle school and growing in more ways than one. She wasn't the little Mya that everyone once knew. She had caramel complexion, long black curly hair, oval shape honey color eyes, standing at 5'4; she even grew up to have hips, breast and now a sassy attitude. She didn't listen to anyone and was doing what she wanted to do. Laurel on the other hand was on a mission to get away from her family. She focused on the

19

books, and didn't let anyone stop her from going to school. Mike hated to see his mother struggle. He dropped out of school and started hustling around Big Mike's old hood. They gave him respect because of his father and the clout he had. Mya... Walking home from school with her best friend Destiny, two high school boys they knew— Scott and Kyle — walked up to them. Destiny was 5'4, brown skin, with long hair that she wore either flat iron or in a ponytail, she had a beautiful smile with a deep dimple and slanted eyes. Destiny was smart and always planned to get out the hood. She was the oldest sibling of two younger brothers and her mother raised them the best she could. "What's up with y'all sexy asses?" Scott said smiling hard. "Scott please! Don't nobody want you." Destiny said rolling her eyes at him. "Shittttt Destiny. All the bitches want me. Ain't that right Mya?" Scott asked but not letting his eyes leave Destiny. Since Scott and Kyle both are brothers they had some similar features but did not look alike. Scott was light skin, 5'9, slim built, pink full lips, light brown eyes, with curly hair, and Kyle was brown skin, 5'11, muscular built, pink full lips, greenish-hazel eyes, with curly hair. Scott took more after his mother, and Kyle took more after his father who was locked up. "If you say so Scott." Mya said shifting her weight to one leg. "So, where are y'all going?" Kyle asked eyeing Mya. With her standing the way she was, her hips stood out more. Kyle already knew what he wanted to do to her. "We going home." Mya responded smiling at Kyle. She had a crush on him for a long time. "Y'all don't want to go over our house?" Kyle asked Mya. "Boy, why would I go to your house?" Mya asked giving him a screwed up face. She eyed him skeptically, not sure of his motive. "Because you know I like you. You gonna to be my girl one of these days." Kyle said grabbing her hand and trying to pull her to him. "Kyle you damn near my brother age." Mya said pulling out of his grip. "What age got to do with anything?" Kyle replied grabbing her hand again and smiling at her. "Destiny is you coming too?" Scott asked, looking at Destiny eagerly. "Hell no, I'm going home." Destiny said beginning to walk in the opposite direction. "So you gonna leave me by myself?" Mya asked Destiny. "No cause your ass ain't going over their house either." Destiny said looking back at her best friend like she was crazy. "Come on for me. We just going to chill and watch TV." Mya said giving her the puppy dog eyes. "Yeah right. We going home." Destiny said. "Kyle tell her why y'all want us to come over." "We just going to watch a movie, order some food and chill. Calm down Destiny. Ain't nobody going to do anything to you. You know you feeling my brother anyway." Kyle said not really caring if she came over or not. Shit, he had other motives in mind with Mya. "No I'm not." Destiny said even though she did have a thing for Scott. "So you don't like me?" Scott asked smiling at her. "Boy please." "So are y'all coming or what?" Kyle asked ready to head to his house. "Yea we coming." Mya said grabbing Destiny's hand and dragging her. Walking into their apartment, their mother was at work so they had the house to themselves. Destiny had a bad feeling about this outing, but wasn't going to leave Mya with them by herself. "Where your mother at?" Destiny asked not wanting to get caught in no boy's house. "She at work. Come sit closer to me." Scott said pulling Destiny closer to him. Destiny and Scott sat on the couch while Mya and Kyle were on the love seat. Kyle pulled out a joint from his pocket and lit it. He puffed a couple of times and passed it to Mya, blowing the smoke in her direction. Mya had never smoked before, so when she tried to mimic Kyle, she immediately started coughing. "Damn girl, take your time." Kyle said patting her on the back. "This ain't no regular shit." "Shut up." Mya said while her eyes were watering. Mya passed the blunt to Scott and he puffed and tried to pass it to Destiny. She easily put her hand up to tell him "no thank you". They smoked two jays and then ate some wings and mumbo sauce from Eddie's carryout that they ordered. "Mya come with me." Kyle said high as hell. "Where are we going?" Mya asked even higher. Her eyes were barely opened and the room looked hazy to her. "Just come on." Kyle said pulling her off the couch and leading her to his room. Alone in the living room, Scott looked at Destiny and grabbed her hand causing her to look up from the TV. "So Destiny... are you going to give me some?" Scott asked with a smirk on his face. He was stroking her hand, slowly inching up her arm. "Hell no." Destiny said ready to smack the shit outta him. "That's why I like you." Scott said smiling at her. "Why is that?" Destiny asked with mad attitude. "Cause you have your own mind. You don't fall for peer pressure and you a good girl." He said nudging her shoulder with his. "Well, if you like me so much, why would you disrespect me and ask if I was going to have sex with you?" Shrugging his shoulders, Scott replied, "It was worth a try. Even though I knew you would say no." "Well, don't ask me that question again." Destiny said sipping her orange soda. "Ok, Miss Destiny, but I do have another question." Scott said leaning closer to her. "What is it Scott?" She asked with an eyebrow raised."Will you be my girlfriend. I'm only 15 and you 13. It's not that much of a difference." He said letting her know that he wasn't that much older than her. Little did Destiny know, he been crushing on her hard for years but was always scared to say something to her. "As long as you don't ask to have sex with me again." Destiny said. She knew she was not ready to have any type of sex yet. "Ok deal. But can I get a kiss as least?" Scott asked. "Yeah you can." Destiny said leaning in and kissing Scott fully on the lips. With Destiny and Scott in the living room, Mya and Kyle were in the bedroom. Kyle had Mya on his twin size bed kissing on her neck, chest, and letting his hands roam all over her. He put his hand inside of her pants, and started to move his finger on her clit. Mya, not ready for his touch, tensed up. "What are you doing?" Mya asked moving back, trying to get his hand out of her panties. "I'm not going to hurt you. Trust me, it's going to feel good." Kyle said. He started to move his finger on and around her clit. He applied more pressure and started massaging it. "Does that feel good?" He asked when he felt Mya loosening up. "Yes it feels great." Mya said moving her hips on his finger, enjoying the feeling. Kyle felt her getting wet. Taking his middle finger, he rubbed around her opening before pushing inside. Mya's body tensed and she let out a little scream. "You ok?" Kyle asked still moving his finger inside of her. "It hurts. What are you doing?" Mya asked turning red. "It's only my finger baby just relax. You want me to stop?" Kyle asked still moving his fingers in her and around her clit. "No, don't stop." Mya said starting to enjoy the feeling of his fingers. Kyle knew it was time to go all the way now since he had Mya wet. "Take all your clothes off." He said pulling his finger out of Mya's tight virgin pussy. Mya took all of her clothes off and lay on her back. Kyle admired her innocent body from her smooth caramel complexion, still developing body, and the nervous look on her face. He knew what he was about to do was wrong but he couldn't help it. Mya was fine and he wanted to get her before any other dude did. Taking his pants and boxers off, he climbed on top of Mya. Grabbing his dick, he teased the head around her opening, trying to get it wet. Without any warning, Kyle rammed his full length into Mya. She screamed loudly, as tears escaped her eyes. Ignoring her cries, Kyle went to work on Mya's virgin body. Lifting her bottom off the bed, he went deeper into her. Arching against him, Mya felt nothing but pain. "Are you ok baby girl?" Kyle finally asked as more tears came out her eyes. "Yes..." Mya said lowly taking all of the strokes that Kyle was giving her even though she wanted to tell him to get the fuck off of her. "You know I love you right?" Kyle said trying to make her relax more. He wanted her to stop crying and enjoy what he was doing. Mya hearing Kyle say that he loved her made her feel like she did the right thing. Mya hadn't heard the words "I love you" in so long, she forgot how it felt to be loved. So naturally when Kyle said he loved her, her heart felt so refreshed. He went on and on with the strokes to Mya's body all the while repeating that he loved her so much. Feeling the soreness between her legs, she didn't want to stop him from making love to her. Kyle felt himself about to cum and pulled out. Jerking his dick, he came on Mya's stomach and thick spurts. "Damn that was good as shit." Kyle said making sure every last drop of cum got on Mya's stomach. "What is this on me?" Mya asked getting nervous. "Girl chill out, it's just cum. I'm about to go get you a rag." Kyle said putting his boxers on and going to get a wet rag. Mya laid there thinking about what she had done and realized that it was fun. Even though her experience was painful, she was happy to have shared it with someone who loved her. Kyle came back and gave Mya the rag. She wiped herself clean and got up to put on her clothes. In so much discomfort, she still managed to get dressed. Kyle looked at his sheets, where he saw blood and said "Damn you came on you period?" "No, I'm not on." Mya said embarrassed to see the blood on his sheets. "Well, where did the blood come from?" Kyle asked, stripping the sheets. "I don't know, but I swear I'm not on my period." Mya said confused by it. Looking over at the clock on his dresser, he noticed the time. "Damn, come on so you can go home. My mom about to get off." Kyle said walking out his room with her behind him. Kyle and Mya walked in the living room to find Destiny and Scott knocked out on the couch. "Yo, Scott, wake up. Ma about to be home." Kyle said kicking Scott foot. Scott woke up and Destiny both stirred from their sleep to see Kyle and Mya standing over them. "Call me tonight." Scott told Destiny after they both had stood and headed to the door. "Ok." Destiny said giving Scott a peck on the lips. "So what happened between y'all?" Kyle asked wanting to know if Scott finally had sex. "Nothing. She my girl though." Scott said smiling. "Oh ok, bro. Alright we see y'all later." Kyle said opening the door for them. "So are you going to call me?" Mya asked excitedly. "Yeah I got you girl." Kyle said smiling. Mya and Destiny left and headed home. Mya was in so much pain walking home that she knew she was walking funny. "Did you do it?" Destiny asked curiously. "Yeah." Mya said smiling. "You know he is not going to call or talk to you no more." Destiny said shaking her head at how dumb her friend could be. Yes they knew them but damn, don't give it up the first time they chill alone. "Yes he will." Mya said hoping her friend was wrong. She figured Destiny was probably mad cause she didn't get to have sex. When Mya made it in the house, her mom was gone to her night job and Laurel was home waiting on her. "Where you been at?" Laurel asked looking up from her math book. "Minding my business." Mya said kicking her shoes off by the door and looking at her sister. "So you think you grown?" She asked closing the book and standing up. "Girl, why don't you just worry about yourself?" Mya said going into the bathroom, ignoring anything else Laurel had to say. Mya ran some hot bathwater and hoped that would take away from the pain that was going on between her legs.

Chapter 4

MYA

Woke up the next day feeling like a new woman. Her body was still sore, but all she knew was that she wanted to do it again. She walked to school with Destiny like she always did and she was so happy when school was over. All she could think about was Kyle during the day. "Destiny lets go find Kyle and Scott." Mya said when she met her outside the school. "I can't go with you today because I got in trouble yesterday for coming in late." She said as she stood on the stairs. "Aww man. Well can you go with me to find him?" Mya asked wanting to see Kyle again. "Sure, come on." Destiny said. They walked around Kyle and Scott's hangout spot looking for either one of them. They finally spotted both of the dudes with their friends on the basketball court. They both walked over to where the group of guys was and caught all their attention. They knew some of them, but not all. "What's up baby?" Scott said to Destiny giving her a tight hug. "Nothing much. Just about to go home."

Destiny said once he released her from the hug. "You not hanging with me today?" He asked giving her a sad look. "I already told you last night I can't." Destiny said rolling her eyes. "I'm sorry for getting you punished. I'm going to take you to the movies when you off of lock down." Scott said causing her to smile. "Really?" She asked with a spark in her eyes. "Yea baby. I do stuff for my girlfriend." Destiny and Scott were in a deep conversation while Mya tried getting Kyle to come and talk to her. "What's up Mya?" Kyle asked. He was irritated with her presence already. Shifting her weight to her right leg, she looked at him and asked, "Why you didn't call me last night?" "I was tired I went to bed. What you want?" Kyle asked in a cold voice. "I wanted to see you." Mya said, feeling hurt about how he was treating her. "So are you coming over here to give me some of that sweet pussy again?" Kyle asked with a smirk on his face. "No." Mya said feeling like she was being used. She couldn't believe this was the same Kyle that was telling her he loved her yesterday. How could he change up so quickly? Looking at her with a screwed up face, he replied, "Well, you can go on and take your young ass home then." "But..." Mya began but Kyle cut her off. "But nothing. If you not giving it up, we don't have anything to talk about." "Well come on." Mya said feeling like she had to sleep with him for him to be around her. "iight fools, I'm out." Kyle said winking at his boys and giving them some dap. "Scott, we about to go to the crib. What you about to do?" Kyle asked his brother. "I'm going to walk Destiny home so I can make sure she safe." Scott said with his arm around her shoulder. Destiny and Scott walked in one direction while Kyle and Mya walked in the other. As soon as they got in Kyle's house, he wasted no time in making her take all of her clothes off. He wanted to turn Mya out, so he dropped his pants and made her get on her knees. Grabbing his dick, he placed it in front of her face. "What are you doing?" Mya asked looking up at him nervously and then at his dick. "You love me right?" Kyle asked still holding his dick. "Yes I love you." "Well suck my dick." Kyle said putting the tip on her lips. "I don't know what I'm doing." Mya said turning her face from his dick that was in her face. "Just put it in your mouth. I'll help you out and don't bite my shit or imma slap the shit out of you." Kyle said Taking a deep breath, Mya gripped his dick and put the tip in her mouth. Kyle wasn't going for it so he slammed his length in till he hit the back of her throat. Gagging and eyes watering, she tried to pull back but he kept his hand behind her head. Kyle didn't care as long as it felt good to him. When he felt himself about to cum he pulled Mya's head closer. Coming in her mouth, he made her swallow it all while she gagged and choked. "Damn that felt good. Good job baby." Kyle said kissing her forehead. Mya just smiled at him while wiping her mouth. He picked her up off her knees and bent her over the couch. Entering her rough from behind, he caused her to let out a painful scream. He went deep inside of Mya. She didn't hide that she was in pain but Kyle didn't care. He kept going deeper and trying to make sure he bust his nut. Not even 3 minutes later, he pulled out and came all over Mya's back and ass. "Damn this pussy gets better and better every time I go up in here." Kyle said catching his breath making sure he got all of his seeds out. Going to get a rag, he came back and wiped her back and ass off, giving it a quick smack. He watched her get redressed and realized that he didn't want her to go anywhere. "Look don't you go out and fuck another dude. This is my pussy. I promise you if I hear you fucking someone else, I'm going to fuck you up." Kyle said grabbing her face and looking her in her eyes. "I won't do that. I love you." Mya said sincerely. "Yeah we will see. Now go on and take your young ass home." Kyle said pecking her lips while grabbing a handful of her ass. "You not gonna walk me home? It's dark outside." Mya said looking out his window and realized the sun went down. "Girl I have to clean up before my mom comes home." Kyle said looking at her like she was crazy. "Ok, well are you going to call me tonight?" Mya asked hopefully. "Yeah I got you." Mya left and headed home. When she got in the house, her mother was home sitting on the couch waiting for her to show up. "Mya Adams where are you coming from?" Liz asked with her arms crossed over her chest. "I'm coming from Destiny's house." Mya said saying the first thing that came to mind. "So you lying to me now?" Liz asked. "No, I was over there." She said, getting scared. "I went over to Destiny's house and her mom said you weren't there. So I'm going to ask you one more time. Where were you?" Liz asked standing up from the couch. Looking at her mother, she replied nervously, "I was at a friend's house." "So you out here having sex?" Liz asked lowly. Mya knew her mother was getting pissed then. She only used that tone of voice when she was extremely mad. "No, I'm not having sex." Mya said lying to her mother. "Well, what the fuck are you out here doing then?" "Nothing I promise." Mya said starting to cry. She knew what was coming and she couldn't even prepare herself for it. Liz moved away from the couch while taking her belt off. Before Mya could even blink, her mother came down on her with the belt. She beat her legs, arms and when Mya tried to turn and run, she beat her across the back. Mya knew she was wrong for coming home late and lying about where she was at. When Liz finished beating Mya, she laid on the floor crying. She was in pain from the sex with Kyle and then the beating her mother just gave her. Picking herself up off the floor, she took a shower and went right to bed. She felt so bad she didn't know what to do next.

Chapter 5

MYA

Mya went through middle school being Kyle's fuck buddy. She was 13 years old, about to graduate middle school when her worst nightmare came true. She was feeling sick one day and didn't know what was wrong. She was vomiting over and over and feeling pain in her stomach. "Mya honey, are you ok?" Liz asked walking in her and Laurel's room. "No ma. My stomach hurts. I think I have the stomach virus." She said looking at her mother. "Ok, well I'm going to let you stay home today. You don't look well either." Liz said kissing her forehead. "Ok." She said laying back down and closing her eyes. "Just eat some soup if you get hungry." Liz called before she walked out the house on her way to work. Mya laid back down and fell asleep when she heard the front door close. She was sleeping well till her phone rang. "Hello?" She answered groggily. "Why you not at school?" Destiny asked. "I think I have the stomach virus." "Or maybe you been fucking too much and is pregnant."

33

Destiny said laughing into the phone. "Why would you say that?" Mya asked not thinking that was funny. "I read that the stomach virus has the same signs as being pregnant." Destiny said stating facts. She was always interested in health and said she was going to be a doctor. Knowing how much her best friend and Kyle were having sex, she wouldn't put it past her to be pregnant. "Well don't say that. I'm only 13." Mya said rolling her eyes as if Destiny could see her. "I'm going to leave school and come over." Destiny said. "Ok." Mya said hanging up and laying back down. Destiny... Destiny left school on her lunch time and headed to Mya house. Destiny was walking past a CVS store when she was heading to Mya's house and decided to stop. She walked in and went to the pregnancy test aisle. She was busy looking at all the test when a sales woman walked up to her. "May I help you with something?" the lady said, wondering why this young girl was looking at pregnancy test. "Which one of these are the best?" Destiny asked ignoring the look the lady was giving her. "Are you old enough to be buying a pregnancy test?" "Bitch, I ain't ask you to worry about my age. Never mind I will take this one." Destiny said grabbing the test. She went to the cashier and paid for it then left. Destiny knocked on Mya's door, waiting for her to open it. Mya finally opened it looking horrible. "Damn bitch you look ugly." Destiny said looking at Mya messy curly hair, and pale face. "Fuck you. What's in the bag?" She asked letting Destiny in and going to sit on the couch. "It's for you. I brought you some ginger ale and this." Destiny said pulling out the test. "What I suppose to do with that?" Mya asked looking confused.

"Bitch, pee on it." Mya snatched the test out of her hand and went in the bathroom. Destiny sat on the couch and watched TV while Mya used the bathroom. When she came back out and sat next to Destiny, she had a blank look on her face. Destiny looked at her and asked, "What did it say?" "It said I'm pregnant." Mya said emotionless. "So what are we going to do?" she asked more nervous than Mya. She knew that having a baby at 13 was going to be hard. "I don't know. I'm going to call Kyle." Mya said, not knowing what else to do. "I'm here for you." Destiny said giving her best friend a hug. Destiny and Mya chilled and watched TV letting their minds wonder and think about what the future would hold.

Chapter 6

KYLE

Kyle was chilling on the court after school waiting for Mya to meet up with him. He told her to come over after she got out of school and that was an hour ago. "Bro, you waiting for Mya?" Scott asked walking up to his brother. "Yeah, she supposed to meet up with me." Kyle said dapping him up. "I talked to Destiny and Mya sick. She at home." Scott said. "Let's go over there then." Kyle said jumping up off the bleachers. "iight let's go." Scott said Kyle really liked Mya, but knew she was too young to be his girl. He thought maybe when she got in high school next year, they could be a couple. He knew Scott could date Destiny because he was one year older than her but Kyle was 17, 4 years older than Mya. When they made it to Mya building, they walked up the stairs and knocked on the door. "Who is it?" Destiny asked. "Girl open up the door." Kyle said. Destiny opened the door and saw Kyle and Scott standing there. "What y'all doing here?" Destiny asked looking behind them making sure none of

37

Mya's family was around. "I came to see you." Scott said pulling her close to him and kissing her on the lips. "Where is Mya?" Kyle asked looking at her and his brother. "In her room. She isn't feeling too good." Destiny said. "So are you going to let us in?" Kyle asked. She never moved to the side to let them in the house. "I don't know because Mya sister will be home soon." Destiny said not wanting to get Mya in trouble. "I don't care." Kyle said walking in the apartment, brushing past Scott and Destiny. He went in Mya's room and saw she was in the bed. "What you doing here?" Mya asked when he walked in her room. "I can't come and check on you." Kyle asked coming to sit on her bed. "I didn't say that." Mya said sitting up, looking at Kyle observing his good looks. "So what's wrong with you?" "I do need to talk to you." "That can wait. I need some pussy. I don't care if you sick or not." Kyle said unbuckling his pants. Even though she knew she shouldn't do it she wanted him too. Mya sat up and took his dick in her mouth and sucked it. She knew Laurel would be home soon, so she wanted it to be quick as possible. "We going to be fast. My sister will be home soon." Mya said pulling his dick out her mouth. "Aight." Kyle said putting his dick back in her mouth. He pulled out her mouth shortly after and pulled her night shorts off. He got on top of her and began fucking her rough and hard. He went for a good 5 minutes before he bust inside of Mya. He pulled out and laid next to her on the bed trying to catch his breath. "What you got to tell me?" Kyle asked looking up at the ceiling. "Well..." Mya said sitting up looking at him. Destiny... Destiny and Scott sat on the front of her and Mya building talking when she saw a familiar face. "Oh shit." Destiny said out loud. "What?" Scott said wondering what was wrong with her. "There go Laurel, Mya's sister." "Oh damn she look good." Scott said looking Laurel up and down. Destiny hit him in the shoulder, "Babe not like that." "What's up Destiny?" Laurel said with her work clothes on. "Nothing Laurel. How was work?" Destiny said stalling so Mya wouldn't get caught. "It was good. Why are you asking me about work?" Laurel asked giving her a questionable look. Destiny never asked her about her job. "I'm just asking. Oh, this is my boyfriend Scott. Scott this is Mya sister Laurel." Destiny said making introductions. "How are you doing Laurel?" Scott said extending his hand to shake hers. "I'm good." Laurel said shaking his hand. "Well aight. I have homework to do, so see y'all later." Laurel said walking towards the door. "Wait Laurel." Destiny said standing up from the stoop. By the time Laurel turned around to face Destiny, Kyle burst out the building almost knocking her over. "Damn watch it motherfucka." Laurel said mugging him. "Fuck you bitch." Kyle said walking off leaving Scott. "What is it Destiny?" Laurel asked pissed now. Destiny looked off after Kyle, eyeing him warily, "I'm sorry, I forgot." "Ok, whateva." Laurel said heading in the building. "What was that about?" Scott asked looking in the direction of his brother. "I don't know. Maybe you need to catch up with him." "Ok." He got up and gave Destiny a hug and headed to find his brother. Kyle.... Kyle walked up the block with so much going on in his head. All he kept hearing was Mya's voice "I'm pregnant". All he knew was that he was 17 and not ready for no kids. "Yo Kyle. What's wrong?" Scott asked catching up with his brother. "She pregnant." Kyle said still walking, not even focusing. "Oh shit! You ain't wrap it up?" Scott asked trying to keep up with his brother's pace. "Naw, I knew she wasn't fucking anybody else." "So what are you going to do?" Scott asked. "I got a plan." Kyle said, his voice laced with determination. "What is it?" Scott asked. "All I know is she not gonna be pregnant for long." Kyle said continuing to walk home.

Chapter 7

KYLE

Kyle had been so stressed out about getting the news that Mya was pregnant. He had no idea what to do really. He couldn't tell his mother and he didn't have a job to pay for an abortion. He liked Mya but he didn't want to be nobody's father yet. Kyle was in deep thought sitting on the front with Scott, when Ashley, one of Kyle friends, and her crew walked up. "Damn Kyle, you look like a lot is on your mind." Ashley said smiling at him. She always thought that he was cute. "Yeah, I do have a lot on my mind. As a matter of fact, I need to talk to you." Kyle said as a light bulb went off in his head. "About?" Ashley asked skeptically. "Just come with me to my house. I don't want to talk out here." Kyle said getting up from his steps. "Boy, don't think you getting any of this sweet pussy." "Girl just bring your ass on." Kyle said leaving Scott and Ashley's girls outside. Kyle told Ashley what he needed her for and came right back outside with his brother and the girls. "What was that about?" Scott asked. "Oh nothing. I just had to holla at Ashley about something." Kyle said nonchalantly. "Well, at least your ass is calm now." Scott said noticing the change in his brother. "Shut up nigga. Let's go play ball." Kyle said walking off towards the courts. "Come on nigga, I need some money." Scott said. Kyle and Scott hustled to get money. They would box, play basketball, shot dice, and play cards. Anything to get money but sale drugs. When they got to the court, it was some boys there that were beefing with their neighborhood. "I know y'all niggas ain't coming on our court." Anthony said stepping to them when they walked on. Anthony and his boys went to school with Scott and Kyle. They often beefed because girls always go after Kyle and Scott and Anthony didn't like that. He wanted to be top dog and have all the girls flocking to him. Not these pretty boys. "Nigga all that shit you talking we can handle this on the court. Put your money where your mouth at." Kyle said. "Get ready to lose, with your bitch ass." Anthony said. It was Anthony and his boy against Scott and Kyle. Everyone from the block was around to see this game. There was no foul calling since they was playing real street ball. After 30 minutes on the court, Scott and Kyle won. Anthony was pissed because he lost $100 to them. "Man fuck this shit. Y'all niggas ain't going to take our money and just roll like that." Anthony said stepping to Kyle. "Nigga, you lost. Take your L like a real man and stop acting like a bitch." Kyle said stepping toe to toe with him. "Bitch? Oh I got your bitch." Anthony pulled out a gun and aimed it at Kyle. Kyle and Scott just stood there because they weren't going to run or punk out. "Yo Ant, put that up. 5-0 right there." His boy said spotting the police. "Man, fuck 5-0, this nigga talk too much shit." Anthony said still aiming the gun at Kyle. "Do what you gotta do nigga." Kyle said stepping closer to Anthony, the gun right in between his eyes. "Ant put that shit up." His boy said louder. Anthony looked at his friend and knew he was serious and put the gun up. "That's what I thought nigga." Kyle said with a smirk. "This ain't over bitch." Anthony said mugging him as he turned away and headed off the court. Kyle and Scott walked off and headed to their neighborhood. Scott was quiet the whole walk to the apartment, but when they got to the front door to the building he stopped Kyle. "Yo, Kyle I got something to get off my chest." Scott said turning towards him. "What's up?" Kyle asked looking at his brother. "That shit you pulled at the courts wasn't cool at all. That nigga could have killed us." "Oh that nigga wasn't going to do shit. Your ass getting soft on me or something?" Kyle asked. "Nigga ain't shit soft about me. I'm just saying you don't know what the fuck he was going to do. You need to stop being a hot head." Scott said stepping to his brother. "Nigga, please. Ever since you got that lil girlfriend, your ass changed and shit. You becoming a lil bitch." Kyle said looking eye to eye at his brother. "Like I said nigga, ain't shit soft about me. I just care about my life. I don't want my mother to have to bury a son either." Scott said walking off leaving Kyle outside. Kyle was really close to his mother, and he knew his brother was right, but he wasn't going to back down from anyone.

Chapter 8

MYA

It's been a few days since she told Kyle that she was pregnant. She knew she couldn't stay in bed all week, so she got up and got ready for school, even though she was still feeling sick. Mya went to school and was doing fine until lunch time. "Hey girl, how are you feeling?" Destiny asked as she sat at the table with Mya and their other friends Brittany and Tamara. "I'm good. My stomach starting to hurt again." Mya said looking at her food. "Damn girl. That baby got you all fucked up." Destiny whispered to her so no one can hear. "Who you telling?" Mya said in agreement. "Oh, I'm not going to be able to walk home with you today because I have to go over grandma house, and Scott going to walk with me." Destiny said smiling from ear to ear. "You suck." Mya said frowning at her friend. "What did you and Kyle talk about? What he say?" Destiny asked biting into her sandwich. "He was mad and left. He didn't say anything." Mya said looking down at her stomach. "Damn he a bitch ass nigga." Destiny said shaking her head. "Don't say that about him." Mya said getting defensive. She may have been upset with Kyle but she still loved him. Rolling her eyes at Mya's naïve behavior, she replied, "Whatever". Mya and Destiny talked some more and headed to their class after lunch. The rest of the day went by fast for them. The bell rung and Destiny was greeted by Scott waiting for her outside. "Hey Scott." Mya said when she and Destiny walked over to him. "Hey Mya, how you feeling?" Scott asked giving her a hug. "I'm ok. Just sleepy." "Ok, you good walking home by yourself?" Scott asked making sure she was straight before they headed off. "Yea, I'm good. See y'all later." Mya said walking off in the opposite direction. Mya was so sleepy. All she was looking forward to was getting in her bed once she made it home. Walking home, she was in her own zone when she saw a group of girls by the corner store. She didn't pay them any mind. "Aye you Mya?" One girl asked when Mya was walking past them. "Yeah." Mya said looking at the girls not recognizing any of them. "So you the one who been fucking my man Twan?" the girl said. "Naw you got the wrong Mya." She said walking off, not in the mood for this shit. As soon as Mya started to walk, the girl hit her in the back of her head. Mya turned around and started fighting her. She was getting the best of the girl, when her friends jumped in it. They stomped, punched and kicked her in the stomach repeatedly. The girls heard sirens while they were laying into Mya and ran. In so much pain, Mya pulled herself up and limped all the way home, bloody and all. "Mya you late." Laurel said when she heard the door opened. She didn't respond right away so Laurel walked out the kitchen. When she rounded the corner, she saw that her sister was holding her stomach with her face smeared with blood. "What the fuck happened to you?" Laurel asked walking to her sister and looking at her face. "I was jumped. I don't even know the girls." Mya said tears streaking down her face. Laurel was about to ask Mya something but there was a knock on the door that interrupted her. "Who the fuck is it?" Laurel asked upset. "It's me Destiny." Laurel opened the door. "What the fuck happened to you?" Destiny asked shocked to see Mya face as she walked in. "I was jumped." Mya said still holding her stomach tightly. "Where was you when this happened?" Laurel asked Destiny with attitude. "Don't come at me like that. I had to go over my grandmother's house. Who did it?" Destiny asked Mya. "I don't know." Mya said. "I don't even know none of the girls." "Don't you remember anything?" Laurel asked. "All I know is the girl said something about Twan. I don't even know a Twan." "I know a Twan." Laurel said grabbing her phone and looking through her contacts. When she came across the name, she dialed and waited for him to pick up. On the second ring he answered. Laurel didn't even give him time to say hello properly. "Twan, what's your girl name and where she from?" Laurel asked through the phone while Destiny and Mya listened. Twan replied to her, trying to figure out what was going on. "Ok, thanks... Naw that lil bitch and her friends jumped my lil sister." Laurel said in the phone. Hanging up, she grabbed her keys and said "Let's go." They walked out the house and headed to Kyle and Scott's neighborhood. When they approached the neighborhood, Mya looked around and pointed the girls out immediately when she saw them. "That's them right there." Walking up on the girls, Laurel asked, "So which one of you is Ashley?" The girls looked around and Ashley stepped forward. "Me and you are?" Ashley asking standing face to face with Laurel. "So y'all jumped my sister?" Laurel asked upset. Destiny and Mya were not too far behind her. "Oh her." Ashley looked at Mya and laughed. "Bitch ain't shit funny." Destiny said walking up, ready to fight. "Look I'm the one that Twan been fucking. Now do something about it bitch." Laurel said to piss Ashley off. Little did Ashley know, Laurel was a virgin and only reason she knew about Twan was because she tutored him. Ashley swung on Laurel and started the fight. Laurel was beating the shit out of her. She might be a bookworm but she was known to beat a few bitches ass. Destiny and Mya was right behind her fighting Ashley friends that jumped in. Even though Mya was still injured from earlier, she got a burst of energy when she saw her sister fighting. Destiny, Mya and Laurel beat the shit out of Ashley and her friends like it was nothing to it. Once again the police sirens were heard and the girls broke it up and ran off in opposite directions. Walking back home with Destiny and Laurel, Mya started to have a sharp pain in her stomach causing her to collapse on the street. "What's wrong?" Laurel asked when she saw Mya on her knees holding her stomach. "I don't know." Mya said looking down and noticing blood coating the middle of her pants. Destiny saw a cab passing and flagged it down. Wasting no time they hopped in the cab and told the driver to head to the hospital. Laurel called her mom and brother to inform them that they were taking Mya to the hospital. Mya was in the room for two hours before they let her mother in the back. "Mrs. Adams." The doctor said. "Yes, is she ok?" Liz asked nervous about Mya. "Yes, she is stable. She had a miscarriage though." The doctor said. "A what?" Liz said shocked by the news that the doctor had given her. All the color drained from her face. "You can go see her now." The doctor informed Liz. "She's going to need bed rest for a couple of days as well as no strenuous activities for at least a week." Liz was pissed off. She had to get herself together before going to Mya's room. Counting to ten and calming down, she walked in her room and saw her 13 year old daughter laying there. "Hey ma." Mya said praying that her mother didn't know about her being pregnant. "So how long were you pregnant?" Liz asked getting right to the point. "I don't know." Mya said looking down at her hands. She was scared as hell to even be in the same room with her mom at that moment. "Well, you are going on birth control. I can't talk to you right now. We will talk when you get home." Liz said leaving the hospital room before she got arrested for beating her child to death. Mya was scared because her mother was too calm. But for that night she just relaxed in the hospital room. She thought over the fact that she was carrying a child. A life that she would never know. A piece of her and Kyle that was now gone. After leaving the hospital, she was so mad she didn't know what to do. Her focus was on how this could have happened right under her watch. She knew she was overly strict with her kids, but she still set examples and expected them to follow. "Destiny, how long has Mya been pregnant?" Liz asked while she headed back to their neighborhood with Destiny in the backseat. "I didn't know Mya was pregnant Mrs. Adams." Destiny lied to protect her friend. She knew that Mya's mom would flip. "So, you sitting here and telling me that she didn't tell you anything. Who is the guy?" Liz kept asking question as she pulled up and parked the car outside their building. "Mrs. Adams, I really don't know anything and I don't know who the guy is. Thank you for the ride, Later Laurel and Mike." Destiny said getting out the car and heading to her building while the family headed to theirs. As soon as Liz got in the house it was like a 20 questions that she asked Laurel and Mike Jr. "So neither of you noticed that your sister was pregnant?" Liz asked walking back and forth as her oldest children sat on the couch looking at her. "No." They both answered together. Liz put her head down trying to think of what to do next. "Ma, calm down. I'm going to find the little nigga that got her pregnant and you won't have to worry about him." Mike said pulling her in a hug. "No, you are not going to get in any trouble." Liz said looking at her son. "I'm good ma. Love y'all I'm out." Mike said leaving out the house. His manhunt officially began when he walked out. "This is too much for me right now. I'm going to bed." Liz said to Laurel as she walked to her room. "Good night ma." Laurel said thinking about the day when she came from work and Destiny and the boy kept talking to her on the front steps and then the other boy rushing out of the building like he heard the news of his life. Destiny... "Destiny is that you?" Destiny's mother Diana asked. "Yes ma it's me." Destiny said walking in her mother's room. "Where you go after leaving your grandmother house?" "I went over Mya's house." Destiny said. "How is she feeling? She still has the stomach virus?" "She was doing better, but she got jumped today after school. Her sister and I took her to the hospital." Destiny said. "Oh my God. Is she good?" Diana asked. Mya was like a second daughter to her. "Yes, she will be fine." Destiny said when the house phone rung. "Go ahead and get it you know it's that Scott boy." Diana said smirking at her daughter. Destiny laughed at her mother and answered the phone. "Hello." Destiny said walking in the kitchen. "Damn, I haven't heard from you since I walked you to your people house." Scott said. "Aw baby you missed me." Destiny said laughing. "Yeah I missed you girl. What you were up too?" "Well when I got home from my grandmother house I went over Mya house. She was jumped after school by some girls from around your way. So me, her and Laurel went over there and beat the shit out them girls..." while Destiny was telling him the story he cut her off. "What? What was the girls' name that jumped her?" Scott asked jumping up off the couch. "I think one of the girl's names was Ashley. Why?" "Ashley... Y'all good?" Scott asked. "Well me and Laurel good, but Mya in the hospital." Destiny said. "For what? I thought you said y'all won the fight." "Yea we won the fight but I think all the fighting and getting jumped got to her. She had a miscarriage." Destiny said. "Damn, that's fucked up. Let me call you back." Scott said. "I will see you tomorrow. I'm tired." Destiny said. "Ok, good night. I love you Destiny." Scott said. "Good night. I love you too Scott." Destiny said hanging up. Scott... Scott hung up the phone and walked in his and Kyle room. "Kyle." Scott said waking his brother up. "What nigga?" Kyle asked looking at his brother over his shoulder. "What the fuck you do, man?" Scott asked getting mad. "What you talking about?" Kyle asked looking confused. "Son, please tell me you didn't tell Ashley and them to jump Mya." Kyle put his head down. He knew the answer without him even having to say it. "What the fuck is wrong with you? Huh?" Scott asked like he was the oldest. "What you mean? I'm too young to be a fucking father, so I did what I had to do." Kyle said. "Since you only worrying about yourself, that girl was jumped and now she laying up in the hospital." Scott said on the verge of punching his brother in the face. Blood or not, Kyle was beyond foul for pulling that shit. Kyle jumped up now, worried. "Is she ok?" Kyle asked. "What do you care? It's your fault she in there." Scott said. "I didn't want them to put her in the hospital. I just wanted them to scare her. I love that girl." Kyle said putting his head in his hands. He knew he fucked up. "Yeah whatever man." Scott said walking out the room. "What hospital she at?" Kyle asked following his brother. He turned around and replied, "She at Greater Southeast." "Fuck, fuck, fuck." Kyle said going back to his bed. Scott didn't want to tell his brother that Mya lost the baby because he wanted him to see Mya for himself.

Chapter 9

LIZ

After leaving the hospital, she was so mad she didn't know what to do. Her focus was on how this could have happened right under her watch. She knew she was overly strict with her kids, but she still set examples and expected them to follow. "Destiny, how long has Mya been pregnant?" Liz asked while she headed back to their neighborhood with Destiny in the backseat. "I didn't know Mya was pregnant Mrs. Adams." Destiny lied to protect her friend. She knew that Mya's mom would flip. "So, you sitting here and telling me that she didn't tell you anything. Who is the guy?" Liz kept asking question as she pulled up and parked the car outside their building. "Mrs. Adams, I really don't know anything and I don't know who the guy is. Thank you for the ride, Later Laurel and Mike." Destiny said getting out the car and heading to her building while the family headed to theirs. As soon as Liz got in the house it was like a 20 questions that she asked Laurel and Mike Jr. "So neither of you noticed that your sister was pregnant?" Liz asked walking back and forth as her oldest children sat on the couch looking at her. "No." They both answered together. Liz put her head down trying to think of what to do next. "Ma, calm down. I'm going to find the little nigga that got her pregnant and you won't have to worry about him." Mike said pulling her in a hug. "No, you are not going to get in any trouble." Liz said looking at her son. "I'm good ma. Love y'all I'm out." Mike said leaving out the house. His manhunt officially began when he walked out. "This is too much for me right now. I'm going to bed." Liz said to Laurel as she walked to her room. "Good night ma." Laurel said thinking about the day when she came from work and Destiny and the boy kept talking to her on the front steps and then the other boy rushing out of the building like he heard the news of his life. Destiny...

"Destiny is that you?" Destiny's mother Diana asked. "Yes ma it's me." Destiny said walking in her mother's room. "Where you go after leaving your grandmother house?" "I went over Mya's house." Destiny said. "How is she feeling? She still has the stomach virus?" "She was doing better, but she got jumped today after school. Her sister and I took her to the hospital." Destiny said. "Oh my God. Is she good?" Diana asked. Mya was like a second daughter to her. "Yes, she will be fine." Destiny said when the house phone rung. "Go ahead and get it you know it's that Scott boy." Diana said smirking at her daughter. Destiny laughed at her mother and answered the phone. "Hello." Destiny said walking in the kitchen. "Damn, I haven't heard from you since I walked you to your people house." Scott said. "Aw baby you missed me." Destiny said laughing. "Yeah I missed you girl. What you were up too?" "Well when I got home from my grandmother house I went over Mya house. She was jumped after school by some girls from around your way. So me, her and Laurel went over there and beat the shit out them girls..." while Destiny was telling him the story he cut her off. "What? What was the girls' name that jumped her?" Scott asked jumping up off the couch. "I think one of the girl's names was Ashley. Why?" "Ashley... Y'all good?" Scott asked. "Well me and Laurel good, but Mya in the hospital." Destiny said. "For what? I thought you said y'all won the fight." "Yea we won the fight but I think all the fighting and getting jumped got to her. She had a miscarriage." Destiny said. "Damn, that's fucked up. Let me call you back." Scott said. "I will see you tomorrow. I'm tired." Destiny said. "Ok, good night. I love you Destiny." Scott said. "Good night. I love you too Scott." Destiny said hanging up. Scott... Scott hung up the phone and walked in his and Kyle room. "Kyle." Scott said waking his brother up. "What nigga?" Kyle asked looking at his brother over his shoulder. "What the fuck you do, man?" Scott asked getting mad. "What you talking about?" Kyle asked looking confused. "Son, please tell me you didn't tell Ashley and them to jump Mya." Kyle put his head down. He knew the answer without him even having to say it. "What the fuck is wrong with you? Huh?" Scott asked like he was the oldest. "What you mean? I'm too young to be a fucking father, so I did what I had to do." Kyle said. "Since you only worrying about yourself, that girl was jumped and now she laying up in the hospital." Scott said on the verge of punching his brother in the face. Blood or not, Kyle was beyond foul for pulling that shit. Kyle jumped up now, worried. "Is she ok?" Kyle asked. "What do you care? It's your fault she in there." Scott said. "I didn't want them to put her in the hospital. I just wanted them to scare her. I love that girl." Kyle said putting his head in his hands. He knew he fucked up. "Yeah whatever man." Scott said walking out the room. "What hospital she at?" Kyle asked following his brother. He turned around and replied, "She at Greater Southeast." "Fuck, fuck, fuck." Kyle said going back to his bed. Scott didn't want to tell his brother that Mya lost the baby because he wanted him to see Mya for himself.

Chapter 10

KYLE

"Kyle and Scott get y'all asses up before you late for school." Keisha their mother yelled. "Ma, we up dang." Kyle said rolling over. "Who the fuck you think you talking to?" Keisha asked Kyle. "No one ma. I'm up." Kyle said getting out the bed. They got dressed so they wouldn't have to hear their mother mouth any more. "Kyle and Scott, make sure you come straight home too after school." Keisha said. "Why? You not gonna to be here." Kyle said looking his mother up and down. "Man chill out." Scott said to his brother. "Don't tell him anything Scott, but we are going to visit your father today." Keisha said. "I don't want to visit him." Scott said. Scott and Kyle's father was locked up. He murdered his best friend when he found out he was making passes at Keisha. "Look, he want to see you boys and we going. Case closed." Keisha said. "Whatever, we out." Kyle said walking out the door leaving Scott. "Later ma. Love you." Scott said giving his mother a kiss on the cheek. "Love you too Scott." Keisha said while shaking her head at her oldest son, who acted just like his father: a hot head. When Scott walked outside, Kyle was sitting on the steps waiting for him. "Nigga took your punk ass long enough." Kyle said. "Man, save that shit. Would it hurt you to tell ma you love her once in awhile." Scott said while they walked to school. "She knows I love her. I don't always have to tell her. Look check it out, I'm not doing the school thing today. I'm going to see my girl." Kyle said. "You are going to see Mya?" Scott asked making sure he was talking about her or not some other chick. "Yea man. I have to make sure she good." Kyle said. "Iight man. Holla at you later then nigga." Scott said continuing to school while Kyle went to the bus stop that led to the hospital. Kyle got off the bus at the hospital. He had to move swiftly so the police wouldn't take him to school for truancy. When he walked into the hospital, he went to the front desk. "I'm looking for Mya Adams?" "She in room 205." The receptionist said not looking up from her computer screen. Kyle went to her room and when he opened up the door it was dark. He walked over to her bed and tapped her. "Mya. Mya wake up." He said shaking her gently. Mya rubbed her eyes and looked at Kyle and said "What you doing here?" "I had to come and check up on you and my baby." Kyle said smiling down at her. "Oh." Mya said turning her head away from Kyle. "What's up? Why you get all quiet on me?" "I lost the baby." Mya said, her voice weak. Even though Kyle wasn't ready for a baby, he was starting to like the fact that Mya was carrying his seed. "Damn Mya. I'm so sorry." Kyle said hugging her tight. "It's ok. The girls that jumped me mistook me for my sister." Mya said. "Huh?" Kyle said looking at Mya confused. "She said I was talking to her boyfriend Twan but my sister is the one that talks to Twan." Mya said. "Oh damn. I'm still sorry Mya." Kyle said knowing it was his fault. "So you skipped school to come see me?" Mya asked smiling. "Yea, I had to make sure my girlfriend was good." Mya blushed and said "So I'm your girlfriend now?" "Yeah you are. We just going to keep it on the low till you at least get to high school." Kyle said "Deal." Mya said happily. That was the best news she had gotten in such a long time. Kyle and Mya watched TV and talked till it was time for Kyle to leave to head home. "iight Mya, I'm about to roll. I have to go see my pops." Kyle said. "Ok, will I see you tomorrow?" Mya asked hopefully. "How long you going to be in here?" "My mom picking me up today so I'll be home." "Cool, I'll call you tonight." Kyle said kissing Mya again then walking out. As he was walking out of the room and heading to the elevator he bumped into a beautiful Hispanic woman and a tall mixed dude with a baseball cap on. "My bad." Kyle said. "Yea it is your bad." Mike Jr said not knowing he was looking at the guy who got his sister pregnant. Kyle smirked and got on the elevator. Mya... Mike Jr and Liz walked into Mya's room. "Hey ma and Mike. What y'all doing here?" Mya asked. "We are coming to pick you up big head." Mike said smiling at his little sister. "I thought y'all were coming later." "I got off early. Let me go find your doctor." Liz said still upset while leaving the room. "So I take it she still mad?" Mya said to Mike when their mother left. "No shit. You fucking 13 years old and was pregnant. She should kill your ass." Mike said with a straight face. "Man whatever." "So who is the nigga that got you pregnant?" Mike asked, looking down at his sister. "Why you wanna know?" Mya asked, grabbing the sheet around her. "Cause I want to know that's why. Don't ask me no dumb shit like "why" again." Mike said getting frustrated. "It's this dude I met." "Give me a name?" Mike asked pressing her. "I don't know his name." Mya said not trying to get Kyle in trouble. "Yea you can keep on trying to protect that nigga, but when I find him he is dead." Mike said dead serious. Mya was about to say something when their mother. "Your doctor will be in here soon to discharge you." Liz said. "Ok. Ma did you bring me some clothes?" Mya asked. "Yea, I shouldn't bring anything since you want to be grown out here having sex and getting pregnant." "I'm sorry mommy." Mya said looking down at her hands. "Who is this boy that got you in that mess?" Liz asked, with her arms folded. "He is just a boy I met." Before Mya could raise her head to look at her mother, Liz smacked her. "What you smack me for?" Mya asked holding her face holding back her tears. Liz was about to say something when the doctor walked in the room. "Well Mya everything checked out you are free to go home." The doctor said, reading over his chart. "Make sure you follow all instructions and take the prescribed medicine, ok." "Thank you." Mya said looking away from her mother. Liz threw Mya's clothes at her and said she would be waiting in the hallway. Mya got dressed and prayed that her mother would not whip her when they got home. The doctor released Mya and the ride back to their apartment was quiet. When they pulled up at their house, Mya spotted Destiny. Liz and Mike walked in front while Mya walked slowly behind them. "Hey Mrs. Adams and Mike." Destiny said looking at Mike who she had a crush on. She knew that realistically nothing would happen between them. "Hey Destiny." Liz said smiling slightly at her. "Hey boo." Mike said to Destiny with a smile. Destiny blushed as Mya approached her. "Get out of lala land." "Shut up fool. How you feel?" Destiny asked looking her best friend over. "I'm fine. A little sore but that's it." Mya said. "Your ass needs to come in the house now." Liz said angrily. "Well I'll see you tomorrow girl. I'm on lock down till she go to work." Mya said laughing slightly. "I already know." Destiny said giving her a hug. Mya walked in the house and went straight to her room. When she finally got comfortable, Laurel walked in the room. Mya opened up her eyes and looked at her sister. "How are you feeling Mya?" Laurel asked sitting on her bed. "I'm okay. Just a little sore." Mya said. "Well I'm here for you if you just want to talk or anything." Laurel said putting her hand on her. "Thank you so much Laurel." Mya said smiling. She reached up and gave her sister a hug. Mya went right to sleep once Laurel left out of the room.

Chapter 11

LIZ

L iz sat on her bed and cried her eyes out. "Lord where did I go wrong with her. I tried and tried to do the best to provide for them. What am I going to do? Lord my children. Help me with them. Mike Jr. is out selling drugs. I don't hear from him for days, sometimes weeks. Mya was pregnant and Laurel is withdrawing more and more from the family. I need help Lord." Liz cried and prayed, feeling so hurt and lost. She finally looked in the mirror and her once smooth skin now had some age wrinkles. Her once long black hair had greyed at the edges. Her slim body was now thicker around the midsection. Liz looked at herself and saw her mother who she took for granted and didn't appreciate. After dealing with her self-pity, she pulled herself together and went to cook dinner. When walking in the living room she was surprised to see Mike Jr. still there. "Hey ma, you feel better?" Mike asked. "Yes I'm good. You hungry?" Liz asked. "Yea I can eat." Mike said watching TV. Liz went in the kitchen and started to cook. She asked Mike, "Where are your sisters?" "Laurel is in her room doing homework and Mya is sleep." Mike said. "Ok." Liz said going back to cooking. It took her an hour to prepare dinner. She went and woke Mya up and told Laurel dinner was ready. As all of her children were at the table, she realized that it had been awhile since she had all three of her children at the dinner table together. "Mike are you leaving tonight?" Liz asked hoping that this time he would stay. "Naw ma. I'm going to spend the night here tonight to make sure everything is good while you go to work." Mike said. "What you mean to make sure everything is good? We don't need no damn babysitter." Laurel asked getting offended. She could take care of the household while her mom was at work. "Clearly y'all do. In case you forgot, our fucking 13 year old sister was just pregnant." Mike said giving Laurel the evil eye. "Both of y'all cut it out. Mike I'm happy you going to help me out. Laurel if you don't have anything to hide then why is it a big deal that Mike is home?" Liz asked looking towards her daughter. "It's not a big deal ma. I just feel like you don't trust me because of something Mya did." Laurel said pushing her food around on her plate. "I do trust you. I just want a close eye on Mya from now on." Liz said smiling at her. Mya just sat there while her family talked about her like she wasn't at the table. After dinner all of the kids played uno and Liz just watched them, enjoying the moment. She had to get ready shortly and head to the hospital for her night job. "Alright Mya you going to school tomorrow. I will be home at 8. Bye." Liz said walking out the door. All of her kids said Bye as she closed the door behind her.

Mya...

"Damn I'm glad that bitch finally left." Mya said to herself. Mya was trying to figure out a way to sneak out the house to go to Destiny's house. She decided to sneak on the phone and call Destiny. "Hello." Destiny said. "Des, come up here." Mya said in a whisper so her siblings wouldn't overhear her. "Why and why you whispering?" Destiny asked. "I will tell you when you get up here and I'm punished that's why. I'm not supposed to be on the phone." "Ok, I'm coming." Destiny said hanging up. Mya heard Destiny knock on the door and Mike answered it. "Destiny you know Mya is punished right?" "Yea but I just want to talk to her for a little. Please Mike." Destiny said pleadingly. "Ok this 1 time." Mike said letting her through. "Thank you." Destiny said walking to Mya's room. "Damn your brother is so damn fine." Destiny said once she walked in her room and closed the door. "Girl please." Mya said waving her off. "Anyway, what is it that you sneaking calling me and got me out of my house?" Destiny asked. "Kyle came to see me today in the hospital." Mya said excited. "Really? When?" "He skipped school and spent the whole day with me. He held me and everything. I think I want him to spend the night with me tonight." Mya said. "Genius, how do you think he gonna to get in here? Your brother is here." Destiny said. Clearly Mya wasn't thinking straight in this case. "That's why I need your help. I need you to call Scott and pass the message and I will get Kyle in." Mya said. "Mya I'm not down with that plan. How about y'all just skip school tomorrow together. Cause Mike will kill Kyle if he sees him in here." Destiny said. "Ok well pass the message for me." Mya said. Destiny was about to respond when Mike walked in the room "Destiny, baby it's time for you to go." "Ok Mike. Mya see you tomorrow and don't make me late either." Destiny said walking out the room.

Destiny...

Destiny walked back in her apartment and her mother Diana was walking out her room. "Where you coming from Ms.?" Diana asked. "I'm sorry ma, but Mya said it was important and asked if I can come over." Destiny said. "Don't let it happen again Destiny." Diana said walking to her room. Destiny grabbed the phone and dialed Scott number. "Hello." Kyle said after answering. "Hey Kyle. Can I speak to Scott?" Destiny said. "Des, where the fuck is your friend at. I told her little ass to call me tonight?" Kyle said getting mad. "She punished and her brother is at her house so he has her on lock down seriously. She wanted me to pass a message to you though." Destiny said. "What is it?" "She want you to meet her at our school tomorrow. She want to skip the day with you." Destiny said. "Bet I can do that... Yo Scott." Kyle called out for his brother. "Hey sexy." Scott said coming onto the phone. "Hey handsome. I just wanted to call you before I go to bed." "Aw that's sweet baby. Good night and see you tomorrow." Scott said. "Good night." Destiny said hanging up and going to bed. The next morning, Mya was ready to see Kyle. She woke up extra early and made sure she looked good to see her man. "You up early." Laurel said. "I know. I'm ready to go back to school." Mya said lying. "Yea whatever. Just keep your little ass out of trouble." Laurel said getting her things together for school. "I will." Mya said smiling at Laurel then grabbed her book bag to leave out the house to meet Destiny. Mya waited outside of the building waiting for Destiny to come out. Destiny walked out with her two younger brothers Darryl and Darren. "You out here early." Destiny said. "I know. I'm ready to see my man." Mya said, then looked at Darryl and Darren and added "Hey my boo's." "Hey Mya." They both said at the same time smiling at her. "Don't try and turn my brothers out." Destiny said smacking her arm. "Girl they too young for me, but when they turn 18 its fare game." Mya said laughing. "That's nasty." Destiny said as they walked the boys to the elementary school. "Whatever. You talk about my brother all the time." "And your brother is older." Destiny said. "Whatever." Mya said shrugging. They got across the street to the boys school, "Y'all don't get in any trouble today and ma will pick y'all up later." Destiny yelled as they both kept walking like they didn't hear her. "I can swear you act like their mother sometimes." Mya said as they walked. "I have to help my mother out. Some of us can't be spoiled and the youngest." Destiny said sticking her tongue out. "Bitch I'm not spoiled." Mya said. "If you asked Mike for anything he will give it to your crazy ass." Destiny said. "Only sometimes. Not all the times." Mya said. "My point exactly. So are you really about to skip with Kyle?" Destiny asked. "Yes. You and Scott should skip with us." "Fuck no. We have a test today and I am not messing up my grades for no one." Destiny said. "Well won't you live some?" Mya said. "You didn't learn from the other times hanging with Kyle. Don't get me wrong Kyle is cool sometimes and my boyfriend brother but he is an asshole. He don't give a shit about you Mya. All he care about is fucking you. You end up pregnant by this nigga and you ready to go back and get with this nigga who probably was the cause of your miscarriage in the first place. Those girls were from his way. Do you not see it." Destiny said stating facts. "He loves me. You just mad cause you with Scott and not Kyle." Mya said getting mad at Destiny for telling her the truth. She didn't want to hear anything bad about Kyle. "Not even. He don't you love, he loves what you do for him." Destiny said looking Mya in the eyes. Mya was so pissed off she stomped away from Destiny. "Who the fuck she think she is. She think she better than me or something. Like she knows everything. She don't know shit. I know Kyle loves me, fuck her." Mya was talking to herself beyond pissed off. Walking she didn't even see Kyle and Scott standing on the corner waiting for her and Destiny. "Damn you walking fast." Kyle said catching up to her. "Oh hey. I didn't see you there." Mya said coming from out her own world. "I can tell." Kyle said looking over her face. "Hey Mya, where is Destiny?" Scott asked. "Fuck her. Let's go Kyle." Mya said grabbing his hand. Scott and Kyle looked at each other and then Kyle said "See you later bro." "Y'all be good." Scott said as he saw Destiny approaching them. Mya and Kyle walked off leaving Destiny and Scott standing there. "Hey baby, what's up with your girl?" Scott asked. "She tripping. I tell her the truth and she get's mad. I told her your brother doesn't love her he just likes to fuck her and she got mad because I told her the truth." Destiny said. "How you know my brother don't love her?" Scott asked. "I know you brother's type. I have cousins that do the same thing that your brother does." "My brother does have feelings for Mya." Scott said. He knew that Kyle at least care for her. "Scott I don't want to get into it with you over their relationship, fuck Mya. I have to go before I'm late for school." Destiny said giving him a peck on the lips and walking inside her school.

Mya...

Kyle and Mya walked to his house in silence until Kyle broke it. "So what's up with you and Destiny?" He asked. "Nothing." Mya said. "For real." Kyle asked. "Well she was just basically saying you don't love me and shit. I'm stupid and all that shit. She doesn't know what me and you have going on." Mya said. "That's no reason to go and diss your best friend. Get off that little girl shit. She was looking out for you. You need to apologize to her because she was just telling you how she sees it." Kyle said. "So you saying the shit she was saying was true." Mya asked. "No but say if we not talking anymore and another nigga is doing the shit that Destiny was hipping you to and you getting all upset with your girl who is telling you some real shit." Kyle said. "Whatever." Mya said. They walked in Kyle house and he knew it was about to be on. "Suck my dick." Kyle said up zipping his jeans and pulling his limp dick out of his boxers and sitting on the couch. Mya got on her knees and placed his limp dick in her mouth. She began to suck him and work her jaws to make him hard. Even though Kyle was her first partner, she began to learn quickly. She was causing his toes to curl and eyes to roll in the back of his head. "Damn Mya. You gonna to make me bust... slow down." Kyle moaned. Mya kept going, not caring what Kyle was saying. Before she knew it, Kyle came in her mouth. Wanting to please him, she swallowed all his cum. "Fuck Mya, that shit was good. Get me hard again." Kyle said to her. Mya started to jerk him off and switched to sucking his dick again to get him hard. As soon as he was hard again he said "Strip." Mya knew not to say anything and took all her clothes off. Kyle pushed her on the couch and climbed on top of her. Rubbing his dick around her opening, Kyle pushed deep inside of her. Mya was still tight and still fit on his dick like a glove. Not heeding to the warning of no activities for a week, Mya winced when he first pushed inside. Kyle was going so deep inside of Mya. She was grabbing his back scratching him up. "Fuccccccccccckkkkkkkkkkkk Kyle. Right there." Mya said screaming his name. The more she screamed the harder he fucked her. "Turn over." Kyle said pulling out of her. Mya turned over with her ass in the air facing him. Kyle went inside her with so much force. The further Mya arched her back, the deeper Kyle went inside her. "Who pussy is this?" Kyle asked as he hit her spot again. "It's yoursssssss...Kyleeeeee shit." Mya said trying to hold back on cumming. When Kyle hit a sensitive spot, she couldn't hold back her orgasm. Squeezing his dick as she came, Mya threw it back to him, feeling the head of his dick swell. "Fuck Mya I'm about to cum." Kyle said as he was reaching his peak. "Pull out. I can't get pregnant again." Mya said snapping out of the climax she just reached. Kyle pulled out and came all over her ass. All she could do was fall face first on the couch. Kyle went in the bathroom and cleaned up. He then brought her a rag so she could clean the cum off her ass. "You good?" Kyle asked. "Yes I'm good." Mya said while putting her clothes back on. "I'm hungry. What about you?" Kyle asked. "Yeah I am too." "I'm going to run to the carryout. I'll be back." Kyle said putting his shoes on and heading out the door. Mya watched TV till she dozed off. Kyle walked back in the house and saw Mya knocked out on the couch. He decided to light a blunt when he heard a knock at the door. "Who is it?" Kyle asked. "It's me Taye." Taye was Kyle's best friend. Kyle opened up the door and gave him dap. "Nigga what the fuck you doing home?" Kyle asked. "Man fuck school. I'm making this money." Taye said looking at Mya sleeping on the couch. "I hear you man. I need to be on that move." Kyle said. "I can put you down with my man. Who's the bad bitch sleep on the couch?" Taye asked. "That's my little boo Mya. She my lil baby." Kyle said smiling at her. "Yo she looks like Pretty boy Mike little sister." Taye said. Kyle started laughing. "Nigga you know that Mutha Fucka will kill you if he finds out you fucking his little sister." Taye said hitting the blunt. "Fuck that nigga. I ran into that lame ass nigga yesterday too. Gave that nigga the look like "what's up" and he kept his bitch ass walking." Kyle said sicing up his interaction with Mike at the hospital. "Son you wild. Fuck slim doe.

We about to be in this money soon." Taye said. "Yea son put me on. I'm done with this school shit. That's some square shit." Kyle said. Mya woke up and looked at Taye with a weird look on her face. Even though Taye was very attractive, dark skin, thick eye brows, low Caesar haircut, honey eyes, and thick lips, she was kind of nervous because he wasn't there when she fell asleep. She didn't see Kyle who went in the kitchen to fix his plate of Chinese food. "Hi." Mya said looking confused. "What's up slim? I'm Taye, Kyle friend." "I'm Mya, where is..." Mya was about to say when Kyle walked out of the kitchen. "You finally up?" Kyle said. "Yeah, I was tired." Mya said. "I could tell. Your food in the kitchen." Kyle said. Mya went to the bathroom to got herself together. Afterwards, she went in the kitchen to eat her three wings and mumbo sauce. "Son your joint has a phat ass." Taye said watching Mya walk to the kitchen. "I know but hands off nigga. That's all me." Kyle said. "No sharing?" Taye asked. "Not this one son. I molded her the way I want her to be." Kyle said. Mya walked out of the kitchen with her food and sat back on the sofa and ate. Taye lit up another blunt and passed it to Mya. She puffed and passed it to Kyle. The three of them got high till it was around 2pm. "Come on Mya." Kyle said grabbing her hands. "Where we going?" Mya asked high as hell. "I want some." Kyle said pulling her to his room. "Your friend is out there." Mya said, looking at him nervously. "Son cool." Kyle said pulling her pants down. He pushed her on the bed and got on top of her.

30 minutes later....

"Damn Mya you got some good as pussy." Kyle said giving her a rag so she could clean her stomach. Cleaning up, she looked at the clock and hurried up and got dressed. "I didn't know school was out already. I have to go." Mya said rushing to get her stuff together. "Chill Mya, you going to be good." Kyle said. "No I'm on punishment and if I am not home in 20 minutes my brother will come looking for me. I don't need him to run into Destiny." Mya said. "I told Scott to tell Destiny to walk here so y'all can talk." Kyle said. "You that scared of pretty boy Mike?" Taye asked when he had walked out to the living room. "How you know my brother?" Mya asked looking at Taye. "Everyone knows that nigga." Mya just looked at him and picked up her book bag and said "I have to go." As soon as Mya was about to walk to the door Scott opened it. "What's up y'all?" Scott said when him and Destiny walked in. Destiny and Mya just looked at each other. "Taye my nigga. What's good son?" Scott said. "Shit, who is the cutie you with?" Taye asked giving Destiny a lustful look. She rolled her eyes not giving him any attention. "That's my girlfriend Destiny." Scott said eyeing Taye like he was crazy. "What's up Destiny?" Taye said, his gaze trained on her hard. Destiny rolled her eyes again at him and looked at Mya and said "You ready to go?" "Yeah." Mya said watching the exchange. "So it's like that Destiny?" Taye said with his arms opened. "Chill out son. I just said that's my girl." Scott said getting mad. Taye wasn't about to disrespect him in his house. "Creep." Destiny said leaving out of the apartment with Mya behind her. They walked to their neighborhood, neither of them saying anything to each other. "Look Mya I apologize for being a bitch earlier." Destiny finally said once they were close to their building. "I'm sorry too. I shouldn't have took it to heart. I know you were just trying to look out for me." Mya said. "Still besties?" Destiny asked as she stood in front of her with a big smile. "Fuck yeah." Mya said. They hugged and kept walking. "I got your homework for you too. I told the teachers you still weren't feeling well." "Thank you. You're a life saver. Want to come over and we do this work together?" Mya ask praying Destiny would say yes. She was so far behind it wasn't even funny. "I don't have a choice. You don't know a damn thing we studying in class." Destiny said as they walked to Mya building. As soon as Mya opened up the door, Mike was there. "I was about to come and look for your fast ass." Mike said. "I'm home on time. What's up?" Mya said. "I just knew you were going to be late so I was going to head out." Mike said. "I'm here. Destiny is going to help me with my homework if that is cool with you?" "Yea y'all good. I have to make a run anyway." Mike said walking towards the door to leave. "Later Mike." Destiny said flirting with him. "See you later Destiny." Mike said smiling back at her. "I wish you stop that." Mya said sitting at the table and pulling out her notebook. "Doing what?" Destiny said doing the same thing. "Flirting with my brother that is like 8 years older than you." Mya said in a duh tone.

"Age ain't nothing but a number." Destiny said singing Aaliyah's song to her. "Yea but he'll have a number in jail." Mya said laughing. Destiny bust out laughing as they began to do their homework.

Chapter 12

TIME'S FLYING

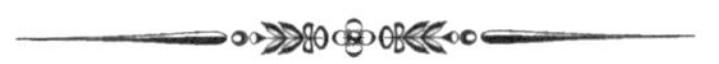

Today was the day that the Adams family was waiting for. Mya was finally graduating middle school and going to high school. "I can't wait to have fun this summer." Mya said to Destiny as they posed for pictures for their families. "Bitch you just got out of school and you ready to get in trouble already. You are a mess." Destiny said smiling for a picture. "I know it is endless that we can do this summer." Mya said, already thinking about the possibilities. "I don't know about you but I will be working this summer." "How? You ain't old enough to work yet?" "Working at my uncle store." "Ask him if I can work too." Mya said, getting excited. "Ok, but you really have to work, not play around." Destiny said. "I'm serious." Mya said "Ok, but I will catch you later. We about to go to dinner." Destiny said giving Mya a hug. "Mya you ready to go?" Liz asked. "Yes." Mya said walking to her family. "Where you want to go out at?" Mike asked. "Outback." Mya said. "Ok deal. Let's go ladies." Mike said to his mother and sisters. They had a great time celebrating Mya's graduation. As soon as Mya got home she was ready to go outside. "Ma can I go outside. I saw my girls at the playground." Mya asked. "Be in here when it gets dark Mya." Liz said. "But ma, it's summer time." Mya said. "I don't care. Have your ass in her when it gets dark." Mya said. "Ma I'm about to go out be back later." Laurel said giving her mother a kiss. "Ok have fun." "How come Laurel don't have to be in when it gets dark outside?" Mya asked. "Because she is older than you and knows how to be responsible." "Whatever." Mya said keeping her voice low so Liz wouldn't hear her. When she got outside she spotted her girls Destiny, Brittany, and Tamara hanging around the playground. Brittany was 5'2, brown skin, shoulder length hair, slanted eyes; some say she looked like Brandy the singer. Tamara was 5'3, light skin, brown eyes round eyes, high cheek bones, and long hair to her shoulders. "What's up ladies?" Mya said as she approached them. "Shit chilling. What took your ass so long to come out here? We saw you pull up." Brittany said. "I had to hear my mother's fucking mouth. What you think?" Mya said. "I saw Laurel come out and get in the car with that nigga from uptown." Tamera said. "How you know he from uptown?" Mya asked. "He's from my cousin's way. I heard that nigga is paid. I ain't know Laurel "Ms. Goodie-Two-Shoes" be hanging with drug boys." Tamera said. "Shit we didn't know either." Destiny said. "Man let's walk around." Mya said. "Bitch you just trying to spy on Kyle ass." Brittany said. "You ain't even slick." "Don't come for me and I'm not. I want to see who's out." Mya said. They all walked around where all the drug dealers hung at. Walking around being fast, they looked at the hustlers that were way out of their league. The older dudes eyed their young bodies as if they were the last piece of meat left. "You see how Cash is looking at me?" Brittany said talking about one of the big drug dealers who was 18. "He ain't even looking at you. He is looking at me." Tamera said matter of factly. "In your dreams." Brittany said. "Both of y'all need to chill because Cash is out of both of y'all league." Destiny said always being the chill one. "Hey Cash." All the girls said at the same time as he walked across the street to where they were. He was heading to the corner store. Cash was dressed to the T. He sported a pair of cargo shorts, blue v-neck shirt, white polo shoes and blue NY hat. A diamond cross chain, diamond's in his ears and a diamond Rolex watch set it off perfectly. Just the way the sun hit his almond complexion, his bright smile with perfect teeth, his slim frame, and his dark eyes, had the girls daze by his sexy features. "Hey ladies." Cash said smiling at them and walked in the store. "His voice, oh my goodness." Tamara said. "Mya ain't that Mike right there?" Brittany said looking across the way. "Oh shit! I have to go. I don't have time for him to embarrass me out here." Mya said walking off the block. "Now that is fineeeeee." Destiny said looking at Mike. Mike was fine as hell, he was 6'6, light skin, oval shape light brown eyes, long curly black hair that he wore in a ponytail or cornrows, muscular frame, and connecting beard. He could dress his ass off too. "Destiny go on with that." Mya said mugging her. "Destiny has a point. Mike is so good looking." Brittany said dreamily. "Whatever." Mya said. They walked around

Kyle and Scott's way. Their block was buzzing since everybody was outside. "Damn their block popping like shit." Tamara said getting a look at everyone that was sitting outside. "I know right." Mya agreed with her. "I see my baby right there." Destiny said walking towards Scott. "Oh goodness." All the girls said together and laughed. "Hey you." Destiny said tapping Scott on the shoulder as he was shooting dice. Scott threw the dice and looked up and saw Destiny and smiled. "Congratulations baby." He said giving her a big hug. "Thank you." "Hey crew. Congratulations to you all." Scott said giving them hugs. They all said thank you to Scott. "So what you doing over here?" Scott asked after gathering his money he won from the dice game. "We were just walking around and came on this end." Destiny said all hugged up under him. "Yeah you were trying to see me." Scott said smiling, showing off his dimples. "Maybe." Destiny said looking away. "Where Kyle at?" Mya asked. "I don't know where that nigga at. Slim supposed to been home two hours ago. He missed our pops visit too." Scott said. All of them chilled with Scott and his homeboys Micah, Shad, and Eric. Micah was 5'9, brown skin, cornrows, medium built, low eyes; he could have past for Omarion. Eric was 5'8, light skin, low haircut, basketball frame, low eyes, and a wide nose. Shad was 5'8, caramel complexion, thick eye brows, long eye lashes, strong jaw line, slanted piercing brown eyes. Even though he was tall and skinny he still was cut. "So what high school y'all go to?" Micah asked. "Why you wanna know?" Tamara asked getting smart with him. "Cause I ain't never seen y'all in my school?" Micah said eyeing her up and down. "What school is that?" she asked. "Ballou." He replied. "I got accepted in Walls." Tamara said proudly. "Damn you one of them smart types huh?" Shad said impressed. Brittany looked between them and said, "We ain't no dumb chicks." "We ain't said that boo." Eric said putting his arm around Brittany. "Boy move your hand." she said. Shad looked at Mya and said "What about you? We know all your girls going to them uppity schools." "I'm going to Walls with my girls." Mya said. "So when am I going to be able to see you." Shad said pulling Mya into him. "What the fuck is going on?" Kyle said appearing out of nowhere. "Oh what's up Kyle?" Shad said trying to give him dap and move away from Mya. "Why your hands on my girl? Mya get your ass over here." Kyle said looking Shad up and down. "My bad son. I ain't know that was you yougin'." Shad said with his hands up. "Yea and keep your hands off nigga." Kyle said then looked at Mya "What I tell you?" "I didn't do anything." Mya said. "Whatever. What's up Scott?" Kyle said finally speaking to his brother. "Where the fuck you been at? You missed the visit to go see pops. Got ma all mad and shit." Scott said angrily. "Man fuck that nigga. I had to make this money." Kyle said patting his pockets. "So now you a fucking hustler?" Scott said. "Chill with all that shit Scott. Yo Mya lets go." Kyle said grabbing Mya's hand. Mya looked at the sky and noticed it was about to get dark soon. "I can't right now. I been over here for the longest but I have to head home before my summer be spent in the house." "Here we go with that lil girl shit. Go ahead and leave." Kyle said snatching his hand away from her. "But Kyle you know how my mother is." Mya said not wanting him to be mad at her. "It's all good Mya, go ahead and head home. I got shit to do anyway." Kyle said nonchalantly. "Are you going to call me later?" Mya asked. "I don't know. I have some business I have to take care of." "Yo Kyle my man let's roll." Taye called from across the street. Destiny looked at Taye and said "Ladies let's roll." She still didn't get good vibes from him. He completely creeped her out. All of them headed back to their neighborhood shortly after. "I will see y'all later. Let me get in here before this lady start tripping on me." Mya said. "Lock down you go." Tamera said laughing at Mya.

Chapter 13

LAUREL...

Even though Laurel was dating one of uptown finest drug dealer's, she kept all her morals. That's what attracted him to her when he first met her at her job at footlocker. "Welcome to footlocker is there anything I can help you with?" Laurel asked. It was a slow day and she was about to get off soon. Loyalty looked up at her and it was like magic between the two. He was taken aback by Laurel's beauty. Her curly long hair was pulled back in a ponytail which enhanced her features: her oval shape brown eyes, full lips, and button nose with the beauty mark on the side. She stood 5'4 with nice round hips and ass. She was so petite that Loyalty thought he could almost break her if he breathed too hard. Laurel looked Loyalty over as well. He had a caramel complexion, 6'2, athletic frame and hazel eyes you could get lost in. What drew Laurel in was the dimple in his left cheek when he smiled and his full pink lips. She already was fantasizing about what those lips would feel like on her skin. Kissing on her neck till he made his way down to her... "Um I'm sorry. What did you say?" Loyalty asked realizing that he was just staring at her. "I asked if I could help you with anything." Laurel said with a chuckle, even though she was just in her own world. "I'm sorry sweetheart. I was just so caught up in your beauty that I didn't hear you." Loyalty said being straight forward with her. "Thank you for the compliment but my name is Laurel not sweetheart. Just let me know when you ready." Laurel said walking away. "Niggas always trying to mack." Laurel said to herself thinking Loyalty was trying to run game on her. "Excuse me Ms. Laurel. I'm ready." Loyalty said smirking at her. "Ok what can I get you?" Laurel asked walking back over to him. "I will take those Jordan's right there, size 11." "Ok I will be right back." Laurel said leaving him to go to the back. Laurel got the shoes and opened the box for him. "Would you like to try them on?" "No I know they'll fit." He said smiling at her. "Will that be it?" "No." "What else can I help you with?" "Your phone number." Loyalty said with his winning smile that he knew girl's couldn't resist. Laurel rung his shoes up and looked him straight in the eye and said "$210 will be your total today." Loyalty paid her and said "So is that a no to the number?" "That's a hell no." Laurel said handing him his bag and change and said "Have a nice day." After the first time Laurel dissed him, Loyalty showed up at the store everyday she worked. She would turn him down every time he asked for her number. Then one day Laurel was getting off and it started to rain while she waited for the bus. "Fuck. When I leave my umbrella it wants to rain." Laurel said mad pulling out her cell to call

Mike to pick her up but got no answer. When she hung up her cell, an all-black Lexus pulled up with tinted windows and 22 inch rims. The passenger side window rolled down and sitting on the driver side was Loyalty. "Hey Laurel. Would you like a ride?" He asked with his winning smile. "This is considered stalking." Laurel said as a rain drop hit her on the forehead. "I'm not stalking you beautiful. I was leaving the carryout and I saw you over her about to get rained on and I figure I could give you a ride." Loyalty said honestly. Another drop hit her and she took a deep breath. Opening the passenger side door, she got in the car. "If you try anything, I will cut you up." Laurel said letting him know she had a blade on her. "I won't ever hurt you." Loyalty said sincerely, driving her home. "So what you have planned today?" Loyalty asked making conversation. "Homework." Laurel said making sure he followed her directions to her house. "So you a nerd." He said with a chuckle. "If because I take my studying serious makes me a nerd then sure, I am a nerd." She said rolling her eyes and looking out the window. Loyalty loved the way she talked back to him and showed so much drive towards her education. "So how old are you Laurel?" "17. I'll be 18 in three months. What about you?" "I'm 19. What high school you go to?" "Banneker. What you do other than stalk me." Laurel said with a smirk. "Real cute, but I'm not going to lie to you. I sell a few things here and there." "I can tell." "How so?" He replied, taking his eyes from the road to glance at her. "I might be all about my books but I have eyes. I really like your name though." Laurel started to lighten up and enjoy her conversation and company. "Thank you.

85

My pops told me he named me Loyalty because all a man has is his word. He always wanted me to remember that." Loyalty said thinking about his father who was killed. "That's so powerful." "Yeah, my dad was my hero." Laurel turned in her seat to fully face him, "What happened if you mind me asking?" "He was murdered when I was 12." Loyalty said. "Sorry to hear that." Laurel said reaching over and grabbing his hand. Even though they just met not too long ago, they had a connection like no other. "So what about your dad?" Loyalty asked, squeezing Laurel's hand slightly. "My dad is locked up and I could care less if he dies in jail or not." Laurel said not wanting to go into details. "Why would you say that?" "That's another story. My building is right there. Thank you Loyalty." Laurel said getting her book bag so she can get out the car as he pulled up. "Laurel." He called out before she could get out the car. "Yes" "May I have your number now?" Loyalty said smiling. "Sure." She rattled off her number to him. "I'll call you later." Smiling at him, Laurel replied, "Ok." After that day they had been spending a lot of time talking on the phone and even went out on a few dates. Loyalty loved the fact that she was determined to make something out her life, still a virgin, and had high morals for herself. Talking to Laurel made Loyalty want to do something with his life. When Mya and her friends saw Laurel get in Loyalty's car, they were heading to his house to have a dinner and movie night. Sometimes they would go out with his friends or her friends, but a lot of times they liked to be alone and enjoy each other's company. Loyalty had his own place and Laurel loved going over there because it was so peaceful. Being around Loyalty always put a smile on her face. "So you happy it's summer?" Loyalty asked. "Yeah but I'll still be busy doing college applications." "Damn around this time next year you going to be leaving me." Loyalty said pulling Laurel closer to him as they laid on the couch. They were relaxing after the delicious meal Loyalty made for them. "Don't think of it like that." Laurel said looking up at him. "You don't understand Laurel. I never loved a woman before. I know this relationship is still new, but I knew I was meant to be with you from the first day I laid eyes on you." Loyalty said holding her closer to him. "I love you too Loyalty but I want to live in the now moment. I don't want to think about when I will be going off to college. Shoot, I might just go to a local college." She said. "No you won't. You going to get into Harvard like you want." He said kissing her cheek. "I'm glad I have your support. I don't get that at home." "Want to talk about it." Loyalty asked. "Today was Mya's graduation. At dinner I wanted to let my family know my plans for college. I told my mom I planned on going to Harvard and she got mad and said I'm not good enough to make it in that college. I have 4.0 GPA, 1600 on my SATs and active in school. I don't know why she so negative. I swear if I could I would leave. If she not fussing at Mya, she fussing at me to watch Mya like I don't have other things to do than keep an eye on my fast ass sister." Laurel vented to Loyalty like she always did. "If you want, you can move in with me. I would love for you to live here. I want nothing more than to go to sleep and wake to you." Loyalty said looking in her eyes. "I would love to but I can't. I've heard the stories of my mother's life and I don't want to be like her." Laurel said reflecting on her mother's life when she moved in with Big Mike as a teenager. She started having babies and gave up on her life, depending on her man to take care of her. "I would never hit you or stop your dreams. Shit we not even having sex." Loyalty said knowing her family's past. "I know but I will pass." Laurel said looking at her watch and realizing she had to get home. "I have to get home. My mom about to go to work and I have to watch after Mya." Laurel said getting up. "Ok." Loyalty said putting his shoes on and heading for the door with Laurel right behind him. They pulled up in front of her building and he got out and opened her door for her. "I'm going to be working tonight so if I don't hit you, I will in the morning." Loyalty said with his arms around her. "Ok. I have to go to work at 3 tomorrow." Laurel said looking into his hazel eyes. "Alright give me a kiss so I can roll from this side of town." Laurel gave him a passionate kiss, biting his lip softly. She knew they could get carried away so she broke it off and walked to her building. While walking up to the front, she saw some of the dudes who wanted her and the chicks that were jealous of her. Laurel didn't care about any of them. She knew that if any of the girls tried it with her, she would beat their ass. Laurel walked in the house and saw Mya was sitting on the couch. Looking up from the TV, she asked, "Where you go?" "I was with Loyalty." Laurel said sitting next to her. "Do momma know you talking to him?" "No and we going to keep it that way or I will tell Mike about Kyle." Laurel said looking her in the eye. "Ok dang." Mya said shocked that she knew Kyle's name.

"Well I'm out of here. You both know the rules. Love you." Liz said heading to her night job. "Love you too." Mya and Laurel said dryly. It was very rare that they hear their mother say she loved them. Not that they were really looking for her to say it. "Laurel, you having sex with Loyalty?" Mya asked her sister once their mother left. "No we are not having sex. He appreciates my waiting for marriage." Laurel said. "You can tell me." Mya asked thinking she was lying. "I did tell you the truth. Anyway I'm about go outside and chill on the front. Tiara is out there." Laurel said. "I'm going too." Mya said getting up and following after her sister. They grabbed the cordless phone, locked up the apartment and went out front. When they got outside, Tiara, Laurel's best friend was outside along with Destiny, Brittany and Tiara little sister Tamara. "Bitch I saw you all hugged up with your nigga. These bitches was hating like shit." Tiara said loudly. "Girl you know I don't pay any of these chicks any attention. They ain't about that life." Laurel laughed. "Laurel let me use your cell." Mya said. Laurel checked her pockets and said "Fuck. I left it in Loyalty car." She picked up the cordless phone and dialed his number. "Hello." Loyalty said sounding like he was smoking. "Didn't mean to bother you but I left my cell in your car. If you not busy, can you bring it to me." Laurel asked. "Yeah baby I will. Give me about 30 minutes." Loyalty said. "Ok thank you." Laurel said. She was about to hang up when Tiara said "Tell him to bring a friend." "Babe, my best friend Tiara said bring a friend with you when you come. We chillin outside." He laughed and said "iight." 30 minutes later Loyalty's car was pulling up. "That car is sexy as hell."

Destiny said eyeing the Lexus. "Ain't it now." Mya said looking at the rims. Loyalty and his best friend Moss got out. Moss was equally as handsome as Loyalty and fresh. He could almost favor the singer Sammie, but he was just finer. "Damn who is he?" Tamara said. "Chill hot ass. That's my boyfriend and his best friend Moss." Laurel said. As Loyalty and Moss walked over they were talking amongst themselves. "I hate this southside area." Moss said mean mugging some of the dudes that were watching them. He wanted any of them to step to him. "Me too, but this where my girl lives and I stay strapped." Loyalty said, touching his gun that was hidden on his side. "Me too man. Is that her friend?" Moss asked as they got close enough to see Tiara. Her bronze complexion, high cheek bones, beautiful smile, shoulder length hair made Moss lick his lips. Even though she was sitting down he knew she was a small thing. As Loyalty told him yea, he eyed Tiara up and down. "Damn she look good." "Hey lil sis, Destiny and Tiara." Loyalty said to them and gave them a hug. "Um Loyalty, that's Tiara's little sister, Tamara and Mya friend Brittany. Y'all this is my boyfriend Loyalty and his friend Moss." Everyone greeted each other. "Here go your phone baby. I can chill with you for a min, but then me and Moss have to hit the brick." Loyalty said. "I understand." "So what you two Spice Girls been up too?" Loyalty asked Destiny and Mya. "Nothing chilling. You know we graduated today." Mya said smiling at Loyalty. "I almost forgot I had gifts for you two." "Where they at?" Destiny said excitedly. "They in the truck. I meant to give them to Laurel earlier but I forgot. We about to leave soon so I'll give them to you when we roll."

He said. Tiara and Moss were talking and laughing on the side. She decided to give him her number since she wanted to feel him out some more. "Moss it's time to roll man." Loyalty said. "I'll hit you later Tiara." Moss said smiling at her and said to Laurel "See you later sis" giving her a hug. "Destiny and Mya come get these gifts." Loyalty said walking to his car. Mya and Destiny were pressed to walk to the car and get their gifts. Loyalty popped the trunk and handed them both gift bags with fresh tennis shoes in them and cards with money. "Did your other two home girls graduate too?" Loyalty asked looking over at their friends. "Yea they did." Destiny replied. Loyalty dug in his pocket and pulled out two hundred dollars and said "Give each of them a hundred and tell them to keep up the good work. Holla at y'all later." "Thank you Loyalty." They both said and headed back to the group. "What y'all get?" Tamara asked when they walked back up. "Oh he gave y'all two this for graduating. We got shoes and cards with $300." Destiny said showing off her shoes. "Hundred dollars? Laurel tell him I said thank you please." Brittany said happily. "I will." Laurel said. They chilled outside for a little longer, just talking and shooting the breeze. After awhile, Tiara and Tamara decided to go home. The group went their separate ways but promised to link back up soon.

Chapter 14

TWO WEEKS OF SUMMER...

———◦→❯❯❯❰❮◦❮◦———

Mya had been working with Destiny and her uncle at his clothing store. She actually had been doing a good job and showing up on time. Since she's been working, her mother loosened up a little and let her have a little freedom. Today was Mya and Destiny's day off, they planned on going to the pool and hang with their girls. "Maaaaaaa." Mya yelled. "What Mya? What do you want?" Liz asked. "Did you see my bathing suit? The new one you just bought me?" Mya asked. "No I gave it to you." Liz said coming into her room. "Nevermind I found it." Mya said finding her new bikini that she was surprised her mother brought for her. She put her bikini on followed by her shorts and a tank top with some cute sandals. She decided to put her long hair in a ponytail to keep it off her neck. "Are you going to the pool? I heard it's a pool party and everyone supposed to be there." Mya said to Laurel who was sitting on the couch. "Naw, I'm about to go to work. Y'all be safe out there." Laurel said texting on her phone. "Ok, well I'm out." Mya said walking out the door to meet up with her friends. "Let's go have some fun." Brittany said when they all met up outside. When they got to the pool party, it was packed. Everybody from every part of the hood was there. They had the radio stations there to broadcast. "This is about to be fun as hell." Mya said excitedly. The girls found some chairs luckily and stripped down to their bikinis, showing off their bodies. They all got in the pool, swimming around and playing. They were having so much fun and enjoying themselves. "What's up sexy?" Scott said walking over to them once they got out the water. He was wearing trunks with no shirt and showing off his six pack and toned chest. "Hey baby. You didn't tell me you were going to be here." Destiny said hugging him. "I wasn't planning on it. My niggas wanted to slide through so I had to make sure none of these niggas trying to get at my girl." Scott said holding her tight. "You know I don't play that. I'm all yours." Destiny said kissing his lips. "Get a room." Mya said to them. "Hey Mya, Brittany, and Tamara." Scott said to each of the girls. "Hey Scott." They all said. "Who you here with?" Tamara asked. "I'm here with my niggas Micah, Shad, and Eric. Kyle somewhere around this place." Scott said looking around. "So Micah on that fake shit?" Tamara said rolling her eyes. "Naw they ain't know I walked off." Scott said spotting his friends walking towards him. "Damn nigga you couldn't tell anyone you walked off and shit." Micah said then looked over at Tamara and licked his lips. "What's baby. Looking good." "I know this." Tamara said rolling her eyes. "Hey ladies." Shad and Eric said and the girls spoke back. They were all chilling when Cash walked by and smiled at them. Every last one of the girls was just staring at him, even Destiny "Damn we ain't sitting here or something." Eric said. "Don't take it personal boo, but Cash just omg." Brittany said causing all the girls to laugh. "Don't get smacked out here." They all went back in the water and swam around for a bit. Getting out the water, they headed to their seats. It started to turn into more of a dance party. The girls put on their shorts and were enjoying the party cause the DJ was killing it. They started to dance and have fun while the DJ blast go-go. "Are you going to dance with me or what Mya?" Shad asked. "I guess me dancing with you won't hurt. Just don't be trying to rub on my booty and stuff." Mya said laughing. They started to dance and have a good time. Across the pool, Kyle was talking to a girl named LaKeisha. "So what's up LaKeisha, you going to let a nigga slide through or what?" Kyle asked smiling at her. "I heard you got a girl and I'm not about that home wrecking stuff." LaKeisha said. "Since when? You just gave me some a couple of weeks ago." Kyle said. "Boy I guess I can see you tonight." LaKeisha said changing up her tune quickly. "Why tonight and not right now?" Kyle asked. "Boyyyyyy." LaKeisha said smiling. "Aye yo Ky." Taye said tapping him. "What son?" Kyle said annoyed he was being interrupted. "Ain't that your girl all grinding up on Shad lil ass?" Taye said laughing. Kyle looked across the pool and saw Shad and Mya dancing up on each other and he got pissed off. "What the fuck?" Kyle said forgetting all about LaKeisha and headed towards Shad and Mya. When he got to them, he grabbed Mya's arm and yanked her

dragged her off and made her leave and my punk ass boyfriend ain't do shit." Destiny said mad as hell. "All that Destiny?" Scott said mad as well. "Yes all of that. You scared of your brother or something?" Destiny asked. "Chill lil sis, don't come at the brother like that. He here to protect you, not Mya. I got this." Loyalty said. "Whatever." Destiny said rolling her eyes. "Watch those fucking eyes little girl." Loyalty said to Destiny then looked at Scott and added "I'm Loyalty. I'm Laurel's boyfriend and this my nigga Moss." "What's up. I'm Scott, Destiny boyfriend and this my niggas Shad, Micah, and Eric." Scott said making introductions. "Nice to meet y'all. Let me go get my little sister before Laurel kills me." Loyalty said walking off toward Kyle and Taye. "Mya." Loyalty yelled her name once they approached Taye and Kyle. "Who the fuck is you and why you calling my girl name?" Kyle said turning around, looking Loyalty up and down. Loyalty laughed at Kyle and said "Slim chill out with that big man stuff. Mya bring your ass on." "She ain't going nowhere slim. Like I said son, who the fuck are you?" Kyle said walking up on him. Mya was so scared she didn't know what to do. Loyalty took a deep breath and clenched his jaw, then said "I'm your worst fucking nightmare and I'm only going to say this one time. Stay the fuck away from Mya?" "And if I don't?" Kyle asked. "You will be floating in the Anacostia River." Loyalty said calmly. Kyle laughed and said "She is mines and she'll never stay away from me." Loyalty just looked at him and looked at Mya and said "Mya bring your ass. We have to go pick up your sister." Mya looked at Loyalty and then at Kyle. Making a sound decision, she started walking towards Loyalty. "Mya." Kyle called out to her. "Yes." She said when she turned around. "I love you." Kyle said, knowing that would make her smile. "Love you too. I'll call you later." Mya smiled, walking off. Loyalty just looked at him and shook his head, while Kyle gave him a gun signal. Loyalty, Moss and Mya walked back to the girls. "Get y'all stuff and let's go." Loyalty said to them. They gathered all their things and gave their boyfriends hugs. Walking out the pool, they followed Moss and Loyalty to their cars. "Moss can you take those three home. We gonna meet up in a hour." Loyalty said. "No doubt." Loyalty opened the door for Mya and then got in. The ride was quiet for a while. "Loyalty you didn't have to do that?" Mya said looking out the window. "Do what?" Loyalty asked. "Come at Kyle like that. I could have handled it." "Mya, now that I talk to your sister, you are my sister and I don't take kindly to seeing MY little sister being dragged across a party by a dumb ass corner boy." Loyalty said. Mya was quiet for a minute not knowing what to say. "Mya, I'm going to talk to you on some real shit. I'm not going to sugar coat it. You can do better than that nigga. I never raised a hand or my voice towards your sister. You don't need a nigga that's treating you like shit. Love ain't supposed to hurt sweetheart. Shit, you young baby girl. You supposed to be out having fun, not worrying about if your boyfriend going to want you going out." He said. "Thank you Loyalty. I'm glad you are in Laurel's life. For a minute, I thought she was a lesbian." Mya said laughing causing Loyalty to laugh as well. "Laurel is definitely not a lesbian." He said shaking his head. "Do you and Laurel have sex?"

Mya asked out the blue. Loyalty almost swerved off the road, "What? What kind of question is that?" He asked looking over at her briefly. "I asked Laurel and she said she still a virgin. But if she dating you and she is always at your house, I know she can't still be." Mya said. Loyalty shook his head and said "Your sister is still a virgin. We've never had sex." "Dang I know that is hard for you. Like, I hear all those girls talking about you and stuff." Mya said remembering how she overheard some girls talking about how amazing he was in bed. "Yeah it can get hard at times and tempting, but I love your sister too much to fuck that up over some pussy. If she wanna wait, then we gonna wait. Ain't no pressure off my end." Loyalty said truthfully. "Wow, where are all the guy's like you. My sister is lucky." "She not lucky. I'm the lucky one." Loyalty said pulling up to Laurel's job. Mya got in the back seat then leaned up and said "Loyalty, can you do me a favor?" "What's up sis?" He asked looking up from his phone. "Can you not tell Laurel about what happened today at the pool." Mya asked him. "She will go off and tell Mike" "I guess it's between us. But if I catch your little boyfriend putting his hands on you again, I will beat the shit out of him." He said with such sincerity. "Ok, thank you brother." Mya said hugging his neck. Laurel got in the car and looked at them weird. "Hey you two." She said. "Hey sis." Mya said kissing her cheek. "Hey baby." Loyalty said leaning over and kissing her on the lips. "So how did you two end up together?" Laurel asked looking between the two. "I saw her and her girls at the pool and offered them a ride. So are you hungry?" Loyalty asked changing the subject. "Yes, but my feet hurt." Laurel said. "We can go get food and go to my place and I will rub your feet." "Thank you baby, but if we take Mya home you know my mom going to make me stay home." "She chilling with us today. I got a good two hours with you." He said kissing her cheek. Loyalty ordered take out from Fridays for them and headed to his condo. "Your house is niceeeeeeeee." Mya said looking around his two bedroom condo. She was amazed at how he had the entertainment center set up with a 65 inch flat screen and the leather sectional. She could see why Laurel spent most of her time over here now. It was too nice not to. "Thanks. Make yourself at home." Loyalty said. "Oh don't tell me that. I will be all through your stuff." "Chill Mya. Act like you've seen a nice place before." Laurel said. "Laurel really? This place shits on our house double time. That's probably why you always over here." "Whatever." Laurel said looking at her phone when it started to ring. "Hey ma, what's up?" She said when she answered. "Where the hell is your grown ass sister?" Liz asked without saying hello. "Mya is with me. She actually met me at work and we having sister time together." "Oh ok. Well I have to do a double tonight at the hospital. I'm about to leave. Do not stay out all night you two." Liz said "We won't." Laurel said hanging up. "What ma wanted?" "She wanted to know where your little ass was at?" "Oh." Mya said, going back to eating her pasta. "She has to work a double tonight." "Good." Mya said, thinking about sneaking Kyle in the house. After they ate, they all sat on the couch and relaxed. Mya went to sleep while Loyalty gave Laurel a foot massage. "Baby that feel so good." Laurel moaned softly. "Anything for you baby." Loyalty said before his phone chimed. He read the text messages and replied. "Baby I have to make a run. Would you and Mya mind staying here till I finish? I won't have time to drop you two off?" He asked. "It's cool. Handle your business." Laurel said. "You are the best." Loyalty said kissing her lips and putting his shoes on. "Just one thing Loyalty." Laurel said, stopping him from leaving. "What's up?" He asked grabbing his keys. "I want to take a shower. Where is everything?" "Baby this is your house too. Snoop around. I Love you." Loyalty said not waiting for a response as he ran out the door. Mya... Laurel just sat there when he told her he love her. He always hinted at it but he never said it before. She felt herself blushing. "Ummmm I see someone over there blushing." Mya said stretching as she got up from her nap. "Shut up. How long you been up anyway?" Laurel asked. "Long enough to hear this is your house and him say I love you." Mya said looking at Laurel smiling. "Whatever big head." There was a brief silence between them. "What am I going to do when you leave Laurel?" Mya asked. "What you mean?" "When you go off to Harvard. Massachusetts is far?" She said looking down. "I might go to a local college. Go to GW or Howard." Laurel said. "You don't want to leave Loyalty?" "That's one of the reasons and I can't leave you to live with momma by yourself. You might drive her crazy." She said laughing. "But Laurel, you always dreamed of going to Harvard. I think you should go." "Thank you Mya. That means a lot." Laurel said hugging her. "Well it looks like we spending the night here, so I'm about to shower. Let me show you where you sleeping and get you some clothes." Laurel said getting up from the couch. Mya followed her down the hall towards the guest room with a bathroom in it. She gave her some of Loyalty's shorts and a shirt, along with a rag and towel. Laurel went into Loyalty's Master room and ran her some bathwater. She found something to sleep in and some under clothes that she had left when she spent the night with him before. She relaxed in the tub and sung to the song that played on the radio. After her bath, she got dressed and went to check on Mya. "Mya you good?" Laurel asked. "Yep, can I use your phone?" She asked. "Yea." Laurel said handing her the phone that was in her hand. She used the phone to call Kyle. He picked up after the 3rd ring. "Who this?" Kyle said when he answered his phone. "Mya." "Oh what's up? You finished hanging with your lil boyfriend?" Kyle said still mad about earlier. "Kyle that is my sister's boyfriend." She said, trying not to make him mad. "Yea whatever. I don't care who he is. If he steps to me like that again, it's over for him." He said. "Where are you?" Mya asked. "Handling business. Why? You trynna come through?" Kyle asked. "I'm actually hanging with my sister right now." "Man whatever. I gotta go." Kyle said ready to hang up the phone. "I can come over tomorrow." Mya said hurriedly. She didn't want him to get off the phone with her so quickly. "If you say so. I'm like last on your list now. What's up with that?" He said trying to make her feel bad. "That's not true and you know it Kyle." "Look man I don't want to argue with you. I'll see you around." Kyle said, not fazed by her words. "I love you." Mya said quietly. "Sure you do." He said hanging up.

Chapter 15

LAUREL

After Laurel checked on Mya, she went back to Loyalty's room and flicked through the channels until she landed on one of her favorite movies "Baby Boy". She was in the middle of saying the movie line for line when Mya tapped on the door. "Come in fool." Laurel said not looking up from the screen. "What you watching?" Mya asked getting in the bed with her. "Baby boy." "That's our shit." She said getting comfortable. "Yep you know it. So what's up with you?" Laurel asked looking at her sister. "What you mean?" "I can tell when something is bothering you Mya." Laurel said looking at her sister and noticing her beauty. Mya and Laurel looked like the younger version of their mother: pure beautiful and all natural. "Well its Kyle. He said I put him last after everyone. But I don't believe it." Mya said playing with the comforter. "I can tell you really love that boy. But at the same time don't be a fool for him either. You have to make yourself happy before trying to make someone else happy. If he feels that way, oh well." Laurel said shrugging. Mya didn't know how to take her sister's comment but knew she knew she had a point. "Thank you." Mya said. By the second movie they were watching, Mya told Laurel she was going to sleep. Laurel was still awake and couldn't sleep so she called Tiara. "What's up trick?" Tiara said answering the phone on the 2nd ring. "Shit what you doing?" Laurel asked. "Girllllll I'm in the house bored as crap. What you doing?" She asked. "I'm at Loyalty house." "I should have known. Trick you always there." "And your point is?" She asked, rolling her neck as if Tiara could see her. "I don't have one." Tiara said. They both shared a laugh. "You so stupid. Anyways, what you doing the rest of the weekend? I'm off." Laurel asked. "Want to go out? I heard TCB playing at the Hot Shops." Tiara said excitedly. She was looking forward to hearing one of the new go-go bands that always got the crowd hyped. "Ugh I guess we can do that." Laurel said not that enthusiastic about it. "Bitch live a little." "Shut up. I'm going to go. How are we going to get there?" Laurel asked. "You should see if Mike will let you drive his car." Laurel frowned her face up and said "You know damn well Mike will not let me use his car. Especially to go to a gogo. I would not hear the end of it and I will def be in the house." "Well I can get my cousin to drop us off and we will have to find a way back home. I'm sure some of the neighborhood niggas will be there so we can get in with them." Tiara said already planning it out. "That's true. So who all is going?" Laurel asked actually getting excited about it. "Me, you and Mel." Tiara said including their other best friend Melanie . "Cool, well let me take my ass to bed. I'll hit you when I'm back around the way." "Alright babes. See you later." Tiara said hanging up. Laurel dosed off, but was woken up to the bed dipping. "Hey." She said half sleep. "Hey baby. I didn't mean to wake you." Loyalty said standing up from the bed. "It's ok. What time is it?" She asked, rubbing her eyes to clear them some. "It's 3 in the morning." He said undressing and getting in the bed, pulling Laurel close to him. "Loyalty how would you feel if I say I'm going to go to local school?" She asked out the blue. "I'm not going to lie baby, I would be so fucking happy. But on the other hand, I would feel like shit cause I know you really want to go to Harvard. Why you ask?" "I just wanted to know. Thank you for supporting me." Laurel said kissing him then snuggling closer in his arms. "You know I got you." Loyalty said kissing the side of her neck. "Oh yea. When school starts back, you get to take me to prom this year." "Baby you know I don't do that prom stuff." "You will this year or I can find another dude to take me." Laurel said smirking. "Shitttttttt, ain't any other nigga going to be up on my woman." He said. He was already thinking about who he would kill if they stepped to Laurel and asked her. "You a mess. Good night baby." "Good night baby. I love you." "Love you too." Laurel said smiling while she drifted off to dreams of Loyalty and her.

Ring, ring, ring...

Laurel's phone rung at 7am, waking her up. "Hello." Laurel said with a raspy voice. "Where the fuck you at?" Mike yelled through the phone. "I'm at umm." Laurel said trying to figure out what to say. She didn't want to let her brother know she was over her boyfriend's house. "Umm my ass. Laurel Mika Adams if you don't have your ass in this house in the next hour it's me and you." Mike said angrily. "Ok." Laurel said rolling her eyes. Mike sure was trynna wear the momma pants today it seemed. "Do you hear me? An hour?" Mike said. "I said Ok damn." Laurel said getting mad. "You acting worse than ma right now." "Watch it. You not too old for me to put my foot in yo ass." Mike said hanging up. Laurel tried to get up but Loyalty had a firm grip on her. "Baby, wake up." Laurel said trying to pry herself from his grip. "What's up baby?" Loyalty said pulling her closer to him. "I have to go. My brother gave me an hour to get home." She said not wanting to get out of his arms. She felt so safe and secure being with him. "iight let's go." Loyalty said letting her go but not wanting to. Laurel got up and went to the guest room where Mya was sleeping wild. She had one leg on the bed while the other was stretched out to the floor. Her head was under the pillow while her arms looked like she was trying to give the bed a hug. "Mya wake up." Laurel said shaking her. "Laurel it's too early." She said turning over. "Mike gave us an hour to get home or it's our ass." As soon as Mike's name left Laurel's mouth, she was up and getting ready. Laurel walked back in the room and saw Loyalty was slipping his sweat pants on. "Do you mind if I keep these? I don't feel like putting my uniform back on." Laurel asked. "Naw ma, you good." He said sitting on the bed trying to wake up fully. "I'm sorry." "Why you telling me you sorry?" He asked pulling her on his lap. Laurel looked down and was about to talk but he grabbed her face so she can look at him. "Always look me in my eyes baby. Now why are you sorry?" "I'm sorry because I can't even spend the night with you without having to go home early. You might think I'm a little high school girl." Laurel said starting to get upset. "Baby I'm not complaining, so why you worried about it." Loyalty said kissing her on the cheek. "I love you so much." Laurel said turning to hug him fully. "I love you more. Now come on before I have to say something to your brother and you will be living with me for real." Loyalty said secretly hoping that would be the case. Mya met them in the hallway after they finished brushing their teeth and washing their face. Loyalty grabbed his car keys and headed towards his car. Opening the door for the ladies, they all got in. He stopped and got them breakfast before heading to their house. "Thank you Loyalty. We have to do this again soon." Mya said getting out the car. "You're welcome lil sis and cool." He said smiling. Laurel looked at Loyalty and took a deep breath. "Guess I'll see you later." Laurel said sadly. She didn't want to leave him just yet. "Baby I will call you after I get some rest. Stop acting like I'm mad or something." Loyalty said laughing at her. "Ok, I love you. Call me later." Laurel said kissing him passionately. "I love you too." Loyalty said hugging her as she made her way out the car. Laurel went in the house and was ready to hear Mike's mouth. "Where the fuck was both of y'all?" Mike asked. "I was with Laurel." Mya said eating her McDonalds hash brown. "We were at my boyfriend house." Laurel said honestly. She figured she had no reason to lie. "When the fuck you get a boyfriend?" Mike asked heated. "We have been together for a while." Laurel said. "Oh so you think you grown to have a boyfriend and shit?" Mike asked stepping to her. "Mike I'm fucking 18 years old. I will be graduating this school year. Yes, I am old enough to have a fucking boyfriend. I'm tired of this shit." Laurel said standing her ground. Mya's eyes got big because Laurel was always the quiet one. She didn't talk back or say much. "So this nigga got you feeling yourself huh?" He said eyeing her up and down. "No he don't but I do everything by the book. I go to school, make nothing but A's, I go to work so I won't have to ask you or momma for shit, I don't go out so I can watch my sister. All I'm saying is I deserve a little fucking piece of mind with my fucking boyfriend without getting cursed out or threatened because I want to spend the night at his house. Damn." Laurel said walking off to her and Mya room's, slamming the door behind her. "Don't slam any fucking doors in here." Mike yelled after her. "Who is this guy she talking too?" He asked Mya who was focused on her breakfast sandwich. Mya looked up at him with her mouth full thinking if she should tell him the truth or not. She thought about her sister knowing about Kyle, so decided to keep Loyalty's name a secret. "I don't know the guy." Mya said grabbing her McDonald's bag and making a dash out of the living room to the room with the quickness. "They must think I'm dumb or something." Mike said to himself. "We'll see."

12pm...

Everyone woke up from their naps since it was an early morning for them. Liz was home from work also but was heading to bed. Mya got dressed in some high waist shorts with a half shirt and some chuck Taylors on. She was on her way to see Kyle. She missed him, even though she just saw him yesterday. "Where the fuck you going dressed like that?" Mike asked sitting on the couch. She jumped when she heard him. She hadn't seen him when she walked into the room. "I'm going outside." Mya said. "Not dressed like that. Go change." "Are you serious?" She asked not wanting to change her outfit. She knew she looked cute. "Well stay in the house then." Mya didn't want to stay in the house with her brother and mother. They would drive her crazy. She stomped off to the room and changed. Laurel looked up from her phone and said "I thought you were gone." "I would have been if your brother didn't make me change my outfit." She said looking for something to wear. "You look cute though." Laurel said going back to texting on her phone. "Looked cute." She said changing her outfit to something Mike would be ok with. When she re-dressed, she left so she could walk to Kyle's house. When she got to the front of his building, she saw him hugged up with a girl. Mya was so hurt and didn't know what to do. Sucking up her feelings, she walked up to them. "Hey Kyle." Mya said eyeing the girl but speaking to him. He looked at Mya smiled, "What's up Mya? What you doing here?" "I came to see you, my boyfriend but I get here and see you all up on this hoe ass bitch." Mya said looking the girl up and down. "Hoe ass bitch though?" LaKeisha said pulling away from Kyle. "You heard me." She said ready to give her the hands. "Look little girl. Take your ass back to your part of town before I give you an ass whipping you won't forget." LaKeisha said, stepping to her. "Try me if you want." "Both of y'all chill the fuck out. Mya you should have called and we wouldn't have been going through this. LaKeisha you already know I have a girlfriend, so I don't know why you tripping." Kyle said trying to diffuse the situation. "You weren't worried about your girlfriend when I was sucking your dick and riding you an hour ago." LaKeisha said looking at Mya, smirking. Mya's heart broke when she heard that. She felt tears coming to the surface but she wouldn't let them fall. Not in front of these two. "You know what. You can have him. I don't want him. I can do so much better. Fuck you Kyle." Mya said walking off. "Yo Mya, come here. Mya." Kyle yelled as she kept walking.

Kyle...

"Why the fuck would you tell her that?" Kyle asked LaKeisha getting mad. LaKeisha looked at him and felt no remorse. "I just felt she needed to know." "You a dumb bitch for real." Kyle said moving away from her. "Fuck you Kyle." She yelled at him. Walking off, he yelled back to her with a smirk, "You already did." He needed a blunt bad. He walked over to Taye's house. He knew he was home, so when he answered the door, the rest was history.

Mya...

Mya made it back to her neighborhood just in time. All of her friends were outside. She thought about telling them what Kyle did but she didn't want to hear their mouths. She figured she would keep it to herself. "What's up y'all?" Mya said walking up to her group. "Hey chick. Where are you coming from?" Destiny asked. "From Kyle's. Anyway what we getting into today?" Mya ask changing the subject fast. "Going to the basketball court. The tournament is today." Tamara said already dancing around. "Let's go bitches." Brittany said. They all walked over to the court seeing that it was packed outside. The girls posted up and watched all the fine guys walking around. "There go your brother over there with Cash." Destiny said pointing out Mike. "So." Mya said not in the mood to be bothered by her brother. "Why don't we go speak?" Tamara said. "How about we don't. Y'all know how his ass is." Mya said. "Whatever." All the girls said. The game was live. They were playing like it was the NBA. The girls were enjoying the game and looking at the dudes. They were so busy looking at a guy with his shirt off, that they didn't notice Mike walk up to them. "What the fuck are y'all looking at?" Mike said scaring them. "Nothing." They all said smiling. "Don't be smiling at me. Come on." Mike said telling them to follow him to where he and his boys were sitting. "Y'all know my little sister Mya, and her girls Des, Britt, and Tamara." Mike said once they reached his friends. They all said "What's up" but smiled hard at Cash. He just shook his head and smiled at them. Mike and his boys smoked and bet on the game, while the girls enjoyed their time with them. "Ain't that Laurel over there?" Mya pointed out to Mike. "Yea that's her. Go get her." He told her. She got up and walked over to Laurel and her friends Tiara and Melanie. Melanie was 5'4 petite, loc that she dyed blue, brown skin, bright smile, and round brown eyes. "Hey y'all. I didn't know you were coming to the game." Mya said to Laurel. "Yea I didn't plan on it but these fools wanted to come. Who you here with? Thought you were going to see that Kyle boy." "I did but that's another story and I'm here with my girls. Mike said y'all come over there." Mya said pointing to where they were at. "Ugh, alright. Come on y'all. We going over there with my brother and them." Laurel said to her girls. "Damn what's up Laurel?" Cash said as they walked over. He had the biggest crush on her but she would never give him a second look. "Hey Cash, Man, and Reek." Laurel said then looked at Mike and rolled her eyes. "Kill the attitude baby sis." Mike said standing up. He hugged her and kissed the top of her head. "All I get is a hey?" Cash asked not letting her get past him. "Cash what do you want from me?" Laurel asked looking at him. Mya and her friends were listening because they never knew Cash to sweat a girl. But here he was basically begging Laurel to talk to him. Cash got lost in her hazel eyes then said "I just want you to let me take you out one day." Mike shook his head at Cash. He always told him his sister didn't like his fake, pretty boy ass. "Thanks for the offer but I'll pass. I have a boyfriend." Laurel said turning around looking at the game. "Damn, so is it that uptown nigga that drive the all black Lexus?" Cash asked a little jealous. Still looking at the game, she replied, "That's none of your concern." Cash was about to say something else when Mike stepped in. "Cash man leave my damn sister alone." "Whatever." Cash said turning back to the game. It still weighed heavy on his mind how come Laurel wouldn't give him the time of day. Everyone went back to focusing on the game. It was one boy that stood out. He was 16 but was a tall 6'3 playing on the grown men's team and handling them. "Yo that nigga hoopin like shit." Reek said. After the game, Mike called the boy over for a talk. Noticing them, he walked over. "What's up fam?" He said to Mike. "Yo, you did the damn thing my nigga. Cause of you I'm 3000 up so here you go. Keep that shit up all summer and you will be good." Mike said handing him 500. "Thanks." He said looking at the money. "I'm Mike. This Cash, Reek and Man." Mike said introducing them. "I'm Lord. And before you say anything, yes that's my real name." He said then looked at Mya who was walking up to Mike. "Mike, ummmm." Mya said but was lost for words when she saw Lord up close. He was 6'3, caramel complexion, hazel eyes, waves in his hair, muscular frame, and a million dollar smile. "Mya what the hell you want?" Mike asked getting annoyed that she was just staring. "Um, I was just going to ask you can I have some money." Mya said still looking at Lord. "Man here." He said, giving her $100. Picking off another $100, he handed it to her, "And give this to Laurel.... Man, excuse my little sister. That's Mya. Mya this is Lord." Mike said making introductions. "It's all good. Nice to meet you Mya." Lord said putting his hand out so she can shake it. She shook his hand and said "Nice to meet you too Lord and thank you Mike." Mya was about to walk off when Mike said "Be in the house by 10." She looked at him and rolled her eyes. "I'm staying at Tamara house. Ma said it was cool." "Whatever." Mya walked back over to the girls and said "I think I just met my future husband." "Bitch ain't you the one who is all in love with Kyle." Destiny said making the girls laugh. "Well I'm glad we having this sleep over because I have to talk to y'all about him." Mya said. They all went to their own houses and got clothes so they can stay at Tamara's house. When they got there with their bags, Tiara, Melanie and Laurel were already there. "What y'all doing here. What are y'all following us?" Mel asked. "Bitch I live here and ain't nobody following y'all lame asses." Tamara said. "Curse again lil girl and that's your ass." Tonya her mother said coming out her room. "My bad ma. Where you going?" Tamara ask looking at her mother's outfit. "Minding my business, and y'all little asses don't fuck my house up and don't fuck in my house. Are we clear?" Tonya asked everyone. "Yes." They all said together. Once Tonya left, they knew she wouldn't be back till tomorrow. "You got the pack?" Tiara asked Mel. "You already know. Laurel, go and make the drinks so we can be right tonight." Melanie said. "I got y'all. Did you talk to Neda?" Laurel asked Tiara. "Where are y'all going?" Mya asked. "Out and yea she said she will drop us off." The girls had drinks and blunts passed around. Laurel was shocked to see Mya smoke and Mya was shocked to see Laurel smoke. Only person who didn't smoke was Destiny. After they were nice, Laurel, Tiara, and Melanie went and showered and put on their club clothes. Laurel... All of the girls decided to wear high wasted shorts with crop shirts to show off their figures with sandals. Laurel took her long hair and put it in a high bun, with hoop earrings, and put on some red lipstick. Tiara let her curly hair stay in its natural look and hang down her back. She wore pink lipstick and different accessories to go with her outfit. Melanie wore her long locs pinned up and burgundy lipstick, with silver accessories. When they walked out, Mya, Destiny, Tiara and Brittany looked at them. "Y'all look cute." Mya said admiring their outfits. "Thank you." They said simultaneously. "Do Mr. Loyalty know what you have on?" Mya asked cheesing hard. "Actually I haven't talked to him all day, so he good." Laurel said kinda upset. She and Loyalty normally talk 5 times a day, but today after he dropped them off she hadn't heard from him. She even texted him a couple of times. "Anyway, let's go. Neda said she outside. Y'all please behave. I don't want to hear ma mouth." Tiara said walking out the door. "We will." Tamara answered. The girls got in Neda car and started drinking some more. When they got to the hot shops, they were hit and ready to have fun. They got in with no problem. Bypassing all the people in the back, they went straight to the front and started partying.

Loyalty...

Loyalty sat in the passenger seat of Moss' car puffing on a blunt and sipping on a henny bottle. After he dropped Laurel and Mya off this morning, he only got an hour of sleep before he had moves to make all day. He was so busy, he hadn't had any time to call Laurel and now these niggas was dragging him to the go-go. "Man you should just drop me off at home." Loyalty said slightly pissed off for being out. "Son, chill out. I'm pretty sure your shawty going to answer after you finish hanging with you best friends." Moss said laughing. "Fucking with y'all I ain't talk to her all day." Loyalty said taking a swig from the bottle. "This nigga whipped." Kelly, another one of his best friends said. "Fuck y'all." He said drinking some more. When they got in, it was packed. They went and brought a bottle of Hen from the bar, even though they weren't 21. If you had money anything goes. They walked around like they owned the place. Loyalty wasn't really a party person, so he stayed in the back drinking while his boys went to the front and danced with the girls. "Damn you fine. Why you back here?" Some girl said walking up on Loyalty. He just looked at her, drunk some of his liquor and wished his phone wasn't dead right now. He definitely would be texting Laurel. Not in some party thinking about her. "So you can't talk?" The girl asked. "Naw boo I can talk, just don't feel like talking to you." Loyalty said dismissing her. "Whatever." The girl said walking off mad. She was hoping to snag him for the night.

Laurel...

Laurel was feeling her drinks and high. She was having so much fun, she actually started to forget that she didn't talk to Loyalty today. "Girl there go your boo." Tiara said laughing while shaking her ass. "Who?" Laurel asked with her face screwed up. "Cash." Tiara said. As if he could hear them speak his name, he started walking to them. "I do not have time for him. I'm about to go to the bathroom." Laurel said about to walk off. "We gonna need him to take us back. Did you forget?" Melanie said. "Ugh, I do have to pee though." Laurel said walking off. She was pushing her way through the crowd and made it to the bathroom. When she came out, she walked smack into Cash. "You're running from me now?" Cash asked smiling at her. "No, I had to go to the bathroom." Laurel said walking around him to go back to her friends. He grabbed her and pulled her to him trying to kiss her. "Cash get off of me. For real." Laurel said ready to slap him. His grip on her arms prevented her from using her hands. Loyalty... "I know I been drinking a lot, but I could sworn that's my girl that just went in the bathroom." Loyalty said to Moss, looking in the direction the girl went. "Man you tripping. I been all around this joint and ain't seen Laurel." Moss said. Loyalty watched the woman's bathroom. He watched as a dude stood by the door like he was waiting for someone. As soon as the girl that he thought was Laurel came out, he saw the guy grab her. He confirmed it was her when she turned sideways. He saw a clear view of her face. "Where you going son?" Kelly asked looking at Loyalty who had a look of rage on his face. Loyalty didn't say anything. His main focus was the dude who had his hands on his girl. He walked up to them and heard Laurel said "Cash, you drunk. Get the fuck away from me." "Laurel you know how much I want to be with you." Cash said still trying to pull her in to kiss her. "I told you Cash I have a boyfriend. Now get off of me before I tell my brother." Loyalty was fuming. He walked up to them and said "Baby you ok?" "Who the fuck are you?" Cash asked letting Laurel go and sizing up the dude who just walked up. Loyalty just looked at him but didn't say anything. He turned his attention to Laurel and asked again "Baby are you ok?" "Yes baby. I'm fine." Laurel said smiling and happy to see him. Even though she was still a little mad at him from earlier. "So, this your lame ass boyfriend." Cash said laughing then added "Laurel you got to be fucking kidding me. You won't talk to me but you will talk to this motherfucker." "You got something you want to say to me. Cause I'm not about that talking shit." Loyalty said getting heated. "Baby come on. He ain't worth it." Laurel said trying to pull Loyalty but he wasn't budging. "My gun talks for me." Cash said looking to fight him. "I swear you so fucking lucky my girl right here or your ass would be dead." Loyalty said with some much anger behind his voice, "I'll see you round. Uptown faking ass nigga." Cash said looking him straight in the eyes. Loyalty just nodded his head. When it came to fighting and firing his gun he was never scared. He was known for bodying niggas for disrespect and Cash would be no different. He grabbed Laurel and walked back in the direction of Moss and Kelly. Before they made it back to his friends, he pulled her to stand in front of him. "Laurel, what the hell are you doing here?" "Having fun. So you can come out but you couldn't call me all day." Laurel asked with an attitude. "Baby it's not even like that. I been busy all day and my phone is dead." Loyalty said trying to make her understand. "If you say so Loyalty." Laurel said brushing him off. "You mad at me?" Loyalty said pulling her to him and wrapping his arm around her waist. Pulling her closer, he started kissing on her neck, making her arch towards him. "I don't know." Laurel said loving the feeling of being in Loyalty arms and his lips on her neck. "Don't be mad at me baby. Gimme a kiss. I missed you all day." "I missed you too." Laurel said kissing him on the lips.

Loyalty sucked on her bottom lip, causing her to gasp. He was waiting for the opening before he stuck his tongue in her mouth. They were in the middle of kissing when they heard "Damn this don't look like the bathroom but it's better than the show up front." They both stopped kissing and looked to where the voices came from. Tiara and Melanie stood before them with wide grins. "I'm Melanie, since my friend so rude and can't make introductions." She said putting her hand out for Loyalty to shake. "Hey Melanie. I'm Loyalty, her boyfriend. What's up Tiara." He said shaking Melanie's hand and hugging Tiara. "So you the guy who always taking up our girl time." Melanie said folding her arms across her chest. "Yea that's me. My bad." Loyalty said still holding on to Laurel like she would disappear. "Where is Moss?" Tiara asked looking around the club. "He over there. Come on." Loyalty said taking Laurel's hand and walking towards Moss and Kelly. "Where the fuck you go nigga?" Moss asked once they walked up to them. "Man I had something to handle. Look who I found." Loyalty said stepping aside so the girls were in sight. "What's up baby?" Moss said moving towards Tiara. He picked her up and started tonguing her down. "Damn." Kelly said watching as Moss grabbed a handful of Tiara's ass. Loyalty and Laurel laughed. "Kel this my girl Laurel and her friend Melanie and that's Tiara. Y'all this is my nigga Kelly." Kelly was 6'6, tall, skinny, pointy nose, mocha complexion, full lips, round eyes, and curly hair. He was the joker of the group always joking. "Nice to meet you Laurel. You the girl who got this nigga whipped. He was complaining all fucking day about you. "Man my phone, I need to call her", blah blah blah. What the fuck you do to my man?" Kelly asked cracking up. Laurel laughed and said "I didn't do nothing. Baby you was acting like that today?" Loyalty, who was sipping his Hennessey out the bottle, looked down at her and said "I was." Melanie had been eyeing Kelly while he was talking about Loyalty to Laurel. When he finally looked over at her, he winked and turned his full attention to her. "How y'all getting home?" Moss asked once him and Tiara stopped their freak fest of dancing and kissing. "Um well we were going to ride home with some of the neighborhood boys." Tiara said not meeting Moss' eyes. "Fuck that shit. You know damn well I don't want my joint riding with no other niggas." Moss said. "You taking us home?" Tiara asked. "What kind of question is that? Let's go. This shit about to be over and I be damned if I'm in a middle of a shootout." Moss said walking towards the door with Tiara's hand in his. They all walked to Moss' car. Loyalty was starting to feel the henny in his system. He was horny as fuck but knew Laurel wasn't going to lose her virginity to him like this. "Baby you going home with me?" Loyalty asked Laurel while she sat on his lap in the car. He was sucking on her neck in between rubbing on her thighs. The things he was doing to her were making her feel good. She almost let out a moan when his hands started going higher but held it in. "Yes." Laurel said softly, moving her neck to the side so he could have more access. "Moss nigga take us home." Loyalty said going back to sucking on Laurel's neck. "Fuck you think this is, a taxi cab. Nigga I'm taking you to your car and you take yourself home nigga." Moss said causing everyone to laugh. They pulled up to the trap where Loyalty and Kelly cars were parked. "You going with me?" Kelly asked Melanie, biting his lip as he looked him over. "Boy don't think you getting any." Melanie said waving him off. "I ain't say that, you did. I was just asking since your home girls going with my niggas. You can roll with me." Kelly said. "Fine." Melanie said trying to fake like she wasn't trying to go with Kelly from jump. "Y'all be safe." Tiara said once her girls got out the car. "Baby you have to drive. I'm too fucked up." Loyalty said handing her the keys. They got in the car and headed to his house. When they got to his place, he couldn't keep his hands off of her as they walked to his front door. The shorts that hugged her ass, the tight half shirt and her thick legs were driving him crazy. "Dang Loyalty, what you trying to do?" Laurel moaned as they walked in the house. She squeezed her thighs together and could feel how slick she was. "I want you right now baby. I need to feel you. I'm horny as fuck." Loyalty whispered in her ear as they both fell to his bed. "I'm not ready Loyalty." She said, trying to move from under him. Laurel was laying on the bed and Loyalty was over her looking in her eyes. He shook his head and rolled off of her. "Fuck, I'm sorry Laurel." Loyalty said realizing what he just said. "It's ok. I just don't want to do it and you drunk." Laurel said moving close to him. "Baby I'm not being rude or anything but let me handle him before you want to cuddle." Loyalty said trying to adjust his hard dick. Laurel looked down at his hard dick and felt a rush. Before she knew it, she had her hand in his pants. Grabbing his dick firmly, she started to stroke him up and down softly. Loyalty leaned back and closed his eyes, enjoying the moment. "Squeeze it some more baby." Loyalty moaned out. Laurel squeezed his dick some more. She wasn't sure if she was jerking him off right but she could tell he was loving it. His eyes were closed and he was moaning. "Damn Laurel. Right there baby." Loyalty said picturing her riding him. The motion of her hand was what he felt her pussy would be like. He felt his self about to cum when she started stroking him faster. He opened his eyes and before he could tell her to move her hand, he came. "Fuck baby, I'm so sorry. I tried to stop you but my mouth wouldn't work." Loyalty said looking down at her hands that were covered with his seed. "It's ok. Did you like it?" Laurel asked shyly. "Yea, I loved it. You didn't have to do that." He said catching his breath. "I know but it's the least I can do. You just looked too enticing." Laurel said wiping her hands on the towel he handed to her. "Want to take a shower with me. I promise I won't touch you." He said, his eyes low. "Sure." Laurel said getting up from the bed to walk to the bathroom. They stripped and got in the shower together. Washing each other up, Loyalty took the time to admire how perfect Laurel's body was. Unbeknownst to him, she was eyeing his muscular frame as well. Just the thought of sleeping in his arms put a smile on her face. After they finished showering, they prepared for bed. Laurel scooted back to Loyalty's chest while he wrapped his arms around her, falling into a blissful sleep.

Chapter 16

LAUREL...

"Ohhhhhh my goodnnnnnneesssssss..... Oh Loyalty... What are you mmmmmmmmmm, mmmmmmmmm doing?" she moaned. Looking down the bed, she saw that his head was in between her legs and moving back and forth fast. Loyalty didn't answer her. He kept sucking on her clit and rotating his tongue around it. She wrapped her legs around his neck when he started sucking harder. Moving from her clit, he teased her opening with his tongue. Sticking it inside of her, Laurel felt him swirling it all around inside her. When he felt her tense up, he moved back up and sucked her clit back into his mouth. They pressure that he put on it was driving her crazy. "Loyalty... wait baby, oh fuckkkkkk. Wait I think I have to pee." Laurel said, so confused as to what was going on with her body. She tried to pull away from him but he grasped her thighs over his shoulders. He knew she wasn't experienced with sex in any way. He stopped and looked up at her but kept his finger on her clit still making her moan and move around wildly. "Baby, just relax and let it happen. Don't fight it." He whispered into her thigh as he kissed it. "You don't have to pee. That means you hitting your peak. Relax and let me take care of you." He moved his finger from her clit and went back to eating her out. Laurel came four times back to back before she was so drained, she fell right to sleep. She was sleeping so peacefully, she didn't hear Loyalty tell her he was about to go handle some business. When she woke up lost and looking around, she realized she was still at Loyalty's house. Grabbing her phone, she saw she had text messages from her friends, Loyalty, Mike and missed calls from her mother. Text from Tiara: "Bitchhhhhhhhh when u wake up we have to talk about my night..." Reply: "Ok, and I have to tell u about my morning. Text from Loyalty (bae): "Baby I had some errands to run. I'll be back soon and I'll bring u some food. Love you." Reply: "Ok and I love you too" Mike (Big brother): "What is this I'm hearing you were at the go-go all up on some nigga last night? Don't make me fuck some shit up." Reply: "I don't know where you heard that from, but tell your gossiping ass friends to keep my name out their bitch ass mouths." After she replied to all the messages, she called her mother. "Hey ma. What's up?" Laurel said lying back on the pillow. "Your dad wants you all to come visit him today." Liz said straight to the point. "I'll pass. Are you going to work today?" Laurel said changing the subject. "No I'm off today and we are going to see him. So get your ass home." "Ma why do we have to drive 3 hours away to see a man who don't mean shit to us." She said not meaning to curse at her mother.

"Because he is your damn father. Now you and your sister need to get home." Liz said angrily. Laurel rolled her eyes and said "ok." After hanging up with her mother, she called Loyalty. "Hello." Loyalty said on the 1st ring. "Hey baby. When you coming home?" She asked. "I'm about to pull up in 10 minutes. What's up?" "I have to go see my dad. My mom is insisting, so I have to go back to Tiara's house to get dressed." "Ok. You can come out in 10 minutes." Laurel hung up and took a quick shower and put on a pair of his sweats and tee shirt. When she got dressed, her phone was ringing. "Baby I'm coming now. I had to take a shower." Laurel said rushing. "Ok. Use your key to make sure you lock up." Loyalty reminded her. Laurel laughed and said "I know." She got in the car and Loyalty handed her some take out from Long horn steak house. "I thought we could have lunch together but I know you have to see your pops." "I wish I didn't have to. I don't have nothing to say to him, but I'm coming over tonight." "Ok. How was your morning?" Loyalty asked smirking at her. Laurel blushed and said "It was great. Can you do that again?" Licking his lips, he looked over to her and smiled, "That's no question." Pulling up to Tiara's building, she leaned over and gave him a passionate kiss. "I left my clothes in your dirty clothes hamper." "That's cool baby." Loyalty said laughing. Laurel ran into Tiara's house and got dressed fast so that she and Mya could head home. "Mya you ready?" Laurel asked coming out dressed. "Duh, I was waiting on you." She responded with a bored expression on her face. "Let's go then." Laurel and Mya said bye to their friends and headed home. When they walked through the door, Mike and Liz sat on the couch waiting for them. "Let's get this over with." Mike said not happy about going to see his father either. It was family day at the prison and Big Mike wanted all of them to come up. They got in Mike's car and drove three hours away to the Prison. Laurel shared her food that Loyalty brought her with Mya in the backseat. When they finally got there, it was so packed. "I hate coming here." Laurel said cringing at even going into the building. "Don't we all." Mya said rolling her eyes. They went through the security check and took a seat waiting for the officers to call their name. "Adams." They looked up and waited for their father to come out. Big Mike had gotten bigger from working out so much. His curly hair was now gray. He still had that winning smile and his hazel eyes that all his kids got from him still sparkled. Liz couldn't help but smile at her husband. Even though he beat her ass numerous times, she still loved him. Mya was still a daddy's girl but Mike Jr. and Laurel couldn't stand the sight of their father. "Hey baby." Big Mike said kissing Liz on the lips and hugging her tight. "Hey, you look good." Liz said looking up and admiring her husband's physique. "Thank you. You look good as well." Big Mike said noticing how thick she got. She wasn't the little skinny 16 year old girl he fell in love with. She was a grown woman now. Liz made it her business to dress nice today so he can see what he left at home. "What's up Junior?" Big Mike said looking at Mike. "I would just prefer Mike." He said with a serious face. "Ok, I understand. How my twin doing?" Big Mike said to Laurel. He called her his twin because out of all the kids, she looked the most like him, just lighter. "I'm good." Laurel said dryly and rolled her eyes. "Hey daddy's princess." He turned his attention to Mya. "Hey daddy. I'm good. How you been in here?" Mya asked genuinely concerned. "I'm maintaining. So you ready to start high school?" "Of course I am." She said smiling. Turning his attention back to his oldest daughter, he asked, "Laurel you ready for this last year?" "Yep can't wait." She responded with no emotion at all. Big Mike picked up on her mood and decided to say something. "What the fuck is up with the attitude?" "Excuse me?" Laurel said looking at him like he grew another head. "You heard me. What is up with your fucking attitude?" He asked, getting angry. "Please not today you two." Liz said trying to keep them both calm. They were so much alike in looks and temper. "Naw ma. I'll tell you what's with my fucking attitude. I would rather be any place but here talking to your ass or seeing your face. You want to always have us come up here on family day like we a family. Shit we haven't been a family since I can remember. Your ass was always gone tricking and come home and beat her ass" She said pointing to her mother. "Family my ass. I can't wait to graduate and move to Massachusetts so I won't have to deal with this fucked up ass family." She almost yelled. "So that's how you feel?" He replied, clenching his jaw. "Yes that's how I feel. Mikey let me get the key. I would rather sit in the car than here looking at his face." Laurel said already standing up. Mike Jr handed her the keys. When she looked back at her father, she said, "Oh dad. This will be the last time you ever see me. Take care and have a great life cause I assure you I will." Mike was speechless at what Laurel said. Everyone was actually speechless because again Laurel surprised them with an outburst. "I'm so sorry about that. I don't know what got into her." Liz, said trying to apologize. "Don't apologize Liz. Is that the way all of you feel?" Big Mike asked looking at Mya and Mike. "Well, the only reason I'm here is for ma. I could have been home making money right now. But shit I have to be the man of the family and make sure my ladies made it up here safe. I could have cared less to see you. I been my own man and raised myself for years now. I took care of this family for a while. I never voice my opinion because ma loves to come up here to see you. Why? I don't know, but I will do anything to make sure she is happy and if it's coming up here then so be it." "What about you Mya?" "Well daddy, l love coming to see you and talking to you. I can talk to you about anything." Mya said not wanting to hurt her dad's feelings any more than her sister and brother just did. Even though she would rather be at the mall with her girls. "Well I'm glad to know how my family feels about me. This will be the last family day I expect y'all to be at." "Don't be like that Mike. They love you, you know that. They just are going through a hard time right now. Laurel is trying so hard to get in Harvard and Mike is trying to be the man of the family. They just have a lot going on." Liz tried to explain. "If you say so Liz." Big Mike said looking away from them. Liz, Big Mike and Mya enjoyed the rest of the visit while Mike and Laurel left. They went to get food and hang till they were done. Mya... The ride back to DC was quiet. Everyone was in their own thoughts. As soon as they pulled up in their hood it was live outside. "Ma there go Destiny and them. Can I stay out with them?" Mya asked. "It's already late Mya." Liz said. "Ma please, it's only 8." "Ok Mya." Liz said feeling defeated. Getting out of the car, Mya walked over to Destiny and the girls. "What's up tricks?" Mya said once she reached them. "Bitch you missed all the action around here today." Brittany said. "Shit, what I miss?" She asked. "It was two fights around here. Some of the banger boys tried to come around here and fake on Cash and them, then Cash and them beat their asses." Tamara said. "I'm mad I missed that." Mya said when she saw Lord walking towards them. "Hey what's up Mya?" Lord said smiling down at her. "Hey Lord." Mya said blushing. "I didn't know you live over here." "Yea for a while. You live over here?" She asked, knowing everyone around her way. "Naw my aunt do. I'm just visiting her. Oh damn I'm rude. I'm Lord and you all are?" He asked directing his attention to the girls. They all introduced themselves to him. "It's nice to me y'all. Well Mya I'm about to jet from around here. Can I get your number or something?" Lord ask nervous that she would say no. "Sure." She laughed, putting her number in his flip phone. While she was talking to Lord, Kyle walked up on them. "Really Mya." Kyle said causing her and Lord to look up. "Kyle." Mya said with a frown. "Who the fuck is this clown ass nigga?" Kyle said shorter than Lord but didn't care. He looked him up and down. Lord looked at Kyle and laughed. He turned his attention back to Mya. "I'll catch you later Mya. You really know how to pick them." He said looking at Kyle. When Lord walked off, Kyle was heated. He got in Mya's face and said "Bitch, so you gonna disrespect me like that?" "Bitch?" Mya said looking at Kyle like he was crazy. "Yea bitch. So is that the nigga you fucking, cause you damn sure ain't fucking me." Kyle said getting in her face. "You musta lost your fucking mind. You the one who cheated on me and last I checked, we were not together anymore. So take your ass back to your little hoe you were fucking yesterday." Mya said shooing him away. "Mya don't play with me. You know that little ass attitude you had yesterday is for the birds. Now let's go to my place." Kyle said about to reach for her. "Kyle, I'm not going to keep doing this with you. I love you and you playing with my feelings. Every time I turn around, it's another girl in my face telling me y'all slept together." Mya said. "Baby those chicks will tell you anything so you can breakup with me. They can try and be with me. You know I love you Mya. Now are you coming with me or not?" Kyle said looking her in the eyes. "Yeah I'm coming with you." Mya said looking at the ground. She knew she was letting him get off easy but she was still in deeply in love. "Mya really?" Destiny said overhearing their conversation. "I'll be back." Mya said walking with Kyle towards his neighborhood. Destiny just shook her head at Mya as she left with Kyle. She loved her friend, but she knew that Kyle was making a fool of her. As soon as they got to Kyle's house, he wasted no time taking her to his room. Not giving her a chance to get prepared, he bent her over his bed and pulled her shorts and underwear down. Entering her without any preparation, he showed no mercy on her. All Mya could do was scream his name and take the strokes he was giving her. When he was about to cum, he pulled out and came on her back and ass. "Mya I love you. Don't let these girls get in your head. I'm you man right?" Kyle asked still catching his breath. "Yea you are." Mya said looking at him over her shoulder. "Well you are going to have to trust me over these jealous ass bitches." Kyle said holding her face looking at her. "I do trust you over them, but you were all hugged up on that girl." "Just because you saw me hugging a girl means I had sex with her?" He asked. "No." "Who do I tell that I love all the time?" "Me." "Who going to be the mother of my children and my wife?" "Me." "Well you need to start acting like it and stand by your man." "I will stand by you." "I know you will. I don't like that nigga you were talking to earlier, so stay away from him." "Ok." Mya said even though she didn't plan on stopping hanging with Lord. She liked himand he was cool. Kyle looked at the time and said "Oh shit, get dressed." Mya knew what that meant, so she got dressed fast and left out as soon as his mother was walking to the building. Mya was walking back to her hood when she heard a horn blow. She turned and saw Loyalty. "Get your ass in the car." Loyalty said sneer. Mya ran to the car and got in. "Where is your ass coming from?" He asked, driving her over to her side. "Ummmmm, I was just walking around." Mya said looking everywhere but him. "You gonna learn the hard way. I told you to stay away from that boy. But hey it's your life little sis." Loyalty said knowing what kind of dude Kyle was. "Where were you heading anyway?" Mya asked. "To pick your sister up." "Oh. Loyalty you really love my sister don't you?" She asked, turning in her seat to him. "Yeah I love Laurel a lot. Why you ask?" "I just was asking. I'm glad you make her happy." "Thanks for your approval." Loyalty said pulling in front of their building. "Thank you Loyalty." She said getting out the car. Mya hugged Laurel before she got in the car with Loyalty. Heading to the apartment, she went straight to the shower and was on her way to bed until Liz called her. "Yea ma." Mya said walking back to where her mother's voice came from. "The phone girl." Liz said. Mya took the phone and said "Hello." "Hey Mya. This Lord. What's up with you?" Mya smiled and walked back to her room. She got in the bed and said "nothing, just laying down. I have to work tomorrow." "Oh ok. So that guy... he was your dude or something?" Lord ask curious. He wasn't trynna step on anyone's toes. "Yea he is. I'm sorry for him being rude." "No need. So since we friends now, when are we going to hang out?" "Whenever you want to." Mya said smiling. Mya and Lord talked on the phone until she fell asleep.

Chapter 17

MYA

The summer flew by and school had started up. Mya and her girls were getting used to high school. She and Lord had developed a great friendship. Whenever she needed someone to talk to, he was the person she called and same for him. Kyle was still doing her dirty but she loved him so much she didn't want to believe it. She was still being naïve to the situation. "Hey Lord." Mya said as she walked to the store for her mother. "What's up boo? Where you going?" Lord asked stopping in front of her. "To the store for my mom. What you doing around her?" Mya asked. "You know I come over here on the weekends, don't fake. Want me to walk with you?" Lord asked hopefully. "Sure." Mya said as they both walked to the corner store. "You coming to my game next week big head?" "You already know with your lanky ass." she said laughing. While they were walking, a girl that had a crush on Lord named Keya said "Hey Lord" smiling at him. "Hey Keya. What's good with you?" Lord said.

"Nothing much. Hey Mya." "Hey Keya." "I will check you later Keya." Lord said smiling at her. "Ok." she said walking off. Mya and Lord continued to walk to the store. "Why don't you talk to Keya? I like her way better than that Hoe Rita." Mya said. "Keya a cool chick and all, but on the good side. At least with Rita I know for a fact I'm getting pussy whenever I call and head on a regular." Lord said honestly. "You so nasty." she said as she walked in the store. "I know you not talking. Every time I call your ass either just left Kyle house or heading there." "Jealous are we?" Mya said picking up the stuff her mother wanted. After she gathered everything, she went to the cashier to pay. "Fuck no. I just don't like that nigga. You my best friend and if I catch his ass in the act with another female, I'm beating the shit out of him." Lord said with a serious face. "Aw you care about me." Mya said, fake pouting. "No shit dummy." Lord said taking the bag so he could carry it for her. As soon as they got back around the way, everyone was outside. It was a nice Saturday and no one wanted to be in the house. "Where you two coming from?" Tamera asked eyeing Lord and Mya. "The store with your nosey ass." Lord said plucking her forehead. "Do not play with me Lord." Tamera said. Mya ran the bag up to her mother and came back outside with her friends. "Where Dest at?" Mya asked. "You already know she's babysitting." Brittany said looking at her nails. "Damn on this nice day. I'm about to tell her bring the kid outside." Mya said pulling out her cell phone and texted Destiny to come outside.

Chapter 18

9 MONTHS LATER LAUREL

———— ❊ ————

It was the day that Laurel had been waiting for all her life. She had one month left in high school. Today she was taking her last final and this test would determine if she would be valedictorian. She wrapped up her test and handed it to the teacher. "Good luck Ms. Adams." Mr. Jones her favorite teacher said. "Thank you Mr. Jones." Laurel said smiling at him as she walked out the class. Laurel was walking to her locker when she heard her name. She turned around to see Tiara. "What's up Tee?" Laurel said getting her work clothes out her locker. "I thought you were off today?" Tiara said. "I was but they called and asked if I can come in. Don't you have class right now?" Laurel asked looking at her friend. "Girl it's Mr. Brooks class. You know he has a thing for me so he let me leave after I bull shitted on his final. Shoot all that matter is school is over and I'm graduating." Tiara said. "A mess. When you picking up your prom dress?" Laurel asked as they went in the bathroom so she could change. "Mines will be ready tomorrow. What about you?" she asked. "I get paid in two days so that's when I will pick it up." Laurel said switching out her clothes. "You paying for your dress?" Tiara asked looking at Laurel with a screwed up face. "Yea, you know ma always crying broke and Mike already paying all the bills." Laurel said. "What about Loyalty?" Tiara asked. "Girl I am not going to ask my boyfriend to buy my prom dress. He already don't want to go to prom but he refuse to let me go with anyone else." "I tell you, men. Moss ass going to tell me he not wearing a suit. He ain't coming to my prom all hood. Not my fault these niggas didn't participate in their high school activities." Tiara said. "You so dumb, but let me run out of here before I'm late." Laurel said heading for work. She made it to work on time. Since she was closing today, she knew it would be long. When 10pm came she was so happy to be off. Her feet were hurting and she was sleepy. As soon as she locked the store up with her manger, the bus was coming. While she took the ride home, her phone rung. "Hello." Laurel said sounding tired. "Dang I ain't hear from my lady all day. What's up with that?" Loyalty said, his smooth voice carrying over the phone. "I'm sorry baby. They called me in for work today and I'm just getting off." Laurel yawned out. "Wait you worked the closing shift? Where you at?" Loyalty asked. He hated when she worked closing and rode the bus. "I'm on the bus baby. I'm good." "Which stop you at?" He asked. "Baby I only have two more stops. You don't have to worry." Laurel said laughing. "Why didn't you call me to pick you up?" "I don't know." Laurel said leaning on the bus window. "Laurel I know you use to doing things on your own, but I'm your man. I'm here to take care of you, provide for you and be there when you working late." He said with a laugh. "I know baby." Laurel said ringing the bell to get off the bus. As soon as Laurel got off the bus she bumped into Cash. "What's up Laurel?" Cash said smiling at her. "Hey Cash." Laurel said walking past him still on the phone with Loyalty. "Cash?" Loyalty said through the phone. "Baby he just spoke when I got off the bus. I'm actually walking in the house now." Laurel said making sure to ease him. Opening the door, her mother, brother, and Mya were sitting in the living room together watching TV. "Hey y'all. Is something wrong?" Laurel asked still holding her cell phone. "No honey why would you ask that?" Liz asked. "Because all three of y'all in the same room and it's quiet." Laurel said eyeing them skeptically. "Shut up punk." Mike said then added "here you got mail." "Hold on Loyalty." Laurel said grabbing the envelope from Mike that had Harvard's name on it. She put her phone between her ear and shoulder and opened the envelope. Dear Ms. Laurel Adams, We the admissions staff would like to congratulate you on being accepted into Harvard University for the fall 2005 semester. We look forward to working with such a young, driven, and prestigious individual. Orientation will be August 20, 2005... "Ohhhhhh my Godddddd. I made it. I made it." Laurel yelled after she read the letter. She started to cry hard while clutching the letter in her hand. "Congratulations baby. I knew you could do it." Loyalty said then added "Call me back later." "Ok." Laurel managed to say between tears. Mya got up and ran to Laurel, hugging her. "Congrats sis. I'm proud of you." Mike hugged her and congratulated her too. Liz just looked at her and didn't say anything. "Are you going?" Liz asked causing her kids to look at her. "Yes, why wouldn't I?" Laurel asked. "Well, as soon as you graduate, you can pack your stuff and move out." Liz said with no emotion to her voice. "What you mean ma?" Laurel asked. She looked at her mother like she had lost her mind. In this case, she felt as though she had. "You're 18 Laurel. You have a week left to find somewhere to live." "But ma, I won't be going to school until August. Where am I supposed to live till then?" Laurel asked frantically. "I don't know. You smart. You just got accepted in Harvard. You'll figure it out." Liz said getting up and going to her room. Laurel looked at her mother walk away and broke down crying. "Mike what did I ever do to her? Why does she hate me so much?" Laurel cried. Mike held her while she cried on his shoulder. Laurel cried herself to sleep, so Mike put her in the bed. He went to his mother's room after putting her to bed. "Ma really?" he asked. "Mike get the hell out of my room." Liz said. "You wrong and you know that. It's not our fault you didn't become the lawyer you wanted to be. You should be happy that Laurel is going to Harvard. Shoot, going to college period. She never had done any wrong, no kids, not on drugs, and a Straight A student. Why the hell would you put her out?" Mike said pissed off. "I can do what I want in my house. If you so worried about her, move her in your place when she graduate." Liz said. "You damn right I will." Mike said slamming his mother's door. After getting the news she would be getting put out after she walked across the stage, Laurel went into depression. Nothing was cheering her up. She was supposed to be happy. She got into the school she wanted to, her prom dress was beautiful, and she was valedictorian. She hasn't told her friends, or Loyalty that she will be homeless in 5 days. It was the day before prom and she was out at dinner with Loyalty, Moss, Kelly, Tiara and Melanie. Everyone was laughing and talking but Laurel just sat there in her own world. "Laurel you good?" Melanie asked. "I'm fine." Laurel said picking with her food. "You sure? Cause you been like this for two days now. And you shouldn't be." Tiara said. Laurel was trying so hard not to break down, but she just couldn't hold it anymore and started crying. Everyone just looked at her confused. "Babe talk to me. What's wrong?" Loyalty said never seeing her look so defeated. "I'm sorry. I just have to go." Laurel said getting up from the table and walking to the bathroom. "Yo, what is wrong with her?" Loyalty asks Tiara and Mel. "I don't know but I will find out." Tiara said getting up and following after her. "Naw I got it." Loyalty said getting up walking to the bathroom. He knocked on the door and said "Laurel open up the door." Laurel opened the door and her eyes were red and puff. "Talk to me." Loyalty said. "I don't understand why my mother hates me so much. I'll be homeless in 5 days. She told me after I read my acceptance letter, after graduation I have to be out of her house. Mike said I can stay with him but he has a one bed room. What am I going to do? She doing all of this cause I want to go away to school." Laurel said tears still streaming down her face. "Stop crying. Excuse my language but your mom is a straight up miserable bitch. You already know you can live with me. That's no

question. If you want, I can get you your own place. It's up to you."
Loyalty said pulling her into a hug. "I don't want to invade your space."
She said sniffling in his shirt. "You so cute. You know my place is already
like yours. And how many times have I asked you to move in with me
anyway?" Loyalty said lifting her chin up so she can look at him. "All
the time." Laurel said smiling slightly. "So, fuck the 5 day period. She
wants you gone, we going to move your stuff now." Loyalty said. "Ok."
Loyalty bent down and gave her a deep kiss. They both walked out the
bathroom and back to the table. "Sis you good? You pregnant or
something?" Moss asked. Laurel just looked at him with a screwed face
then said "I'm good and no I'm not pregnant. I never even had sex
before." "Dang so what you do to this nigga that he is so pussy whipped
without getting any." Kelly asked amazed. "None of your damn
business." Loyalty deadpanned. "Laurel what's up with you though?"
Tiara asked worried about her best friend. Laurel told Tiara and
Melanie what happened between her and her mother. To say her best
friends were pissed off was an understatement. They wanted to actually
cuss her mother out for her. "Aye I need y'all to come with me to Laurel
house to get her shit." Loyalty said to Kelly and Moss. "We got you."
Moss said. After they ate, they headed to Laurel's neighborhood. She
used her key to go in the house. Tiara and Melanie helped her pack her
stuff while the boys carried it downstairs. Mya walked in the house
coming from Kyle's. "What's going on?" Mya asked Laurel who was
moving stuff from their room to the front door. "I'm moving in with
Loyalty." Laurel said. "What? Wait you can't leave. Please Laurel don't

leave me." Mya said about to cry. "I'm not leaving you. I was about to get put out anyway. You can always come and spend the night with me." Laurel said hugging her sister to her. "What am I going to do without you here with me?" Mya asked crying hard. Laurel hugged her sister tighter while she cried when they heard "Who the hell are you niggas in my house?" Laurel and Mya looked at each other and walked to the living room seeing an angry Liz. "Who the fuck is these niggas in my house you two?" Liz asked looking between her daughters. "Ma, that's my boyfriend Loyalty and his friends Moss and Kelly. They are helping move my stuff out." Laurel said. "Hi Mrs. Adams. Nice to meet you." Loyalty said putting his hand out for a shake. She just looked at it and then up at him. Loyalty pulled his hand back and smiled while shaking his head. "Ma, you didn't have to be rude." Laurel said. "Who do you think you talking to?" Liz asked walking further into the house. I'm talking to you ma. You know what, you just fucking mad dad got you at a young age and fucked up your dreams. So to take your anger out, you hate on us for doing something with our lives. Yes I'm moving to Massachusetts whether you want me to or not. You and daddy are the same two selfish motherfuckers. I'm out of here. Here is your key. I love you ma, hope to see you at my graduation." Laurel said walking towards the door. "I have to work that day." Liz said then added "Don't try and bring your ass back when he cheats on you, gets you pregnant and leave you." Laurel stopped walking and looked at her mother with hurt in her eyes. "I'm not you ma. I love you too." When Loyalty and Laurel were finally home alone, she ran a bath and sank into it. Trying to ease the tension in her body, she relaxed back against the wall. Tears streamed down her face without her knowing. Hugging her knees to her chest, she began to cry, till her tears mixed in with the water.

Chapter 19

PROM

L aurel woke up a little depressed. Today was her prom and her mother wasn't there to help her prepare. At least her brother and sister would be there to take pictures with her. Also Tiara's mom said she would take Laurel with them to get her hair, nails, feet and make up done. "Good morning baby. It smells good in here." Loyalty said walking up behind Laurel who was cooking breakfast. He kissed the side of her neck, while wrapping his arms around her from behind. "Good morning. Your plate is ready." "I can get use to this babe." Loyalty said sitting at the table digging into his food. "You don't have a choice." she said joining him at the table. "So what you got planned for today?" Loyalty asked with food in his mouth. Laurel gave him a look then said "Going to get prepared for prom. Duh." "My bad for my table manners but this shit good. But yea, I have to get a fresh cut. I can't be looking like a bum at my baby prom." "Are you at least a little excited?" Laurel asked watching for any signs of excitement on his face. "Kinda. I didn't go to my prom. I didn't even go to my graduation. I told them to mail my shit to me." Loyalty said shrugging. "Wow." They finished eating and had small talk in between. Laurel went to shower, while Loyalty cleaned the kitchen. He was watching TV, when Laurel walked out fully dressed. "Umm babe, my brother about to come up." Laurel said in a low voice. "Huh?" Loyalty said not hearing her. "My brother is about to knock on the door. He wants to talk to you since you two haven't been fully introduced." she said a little nervous. "Ok cool." Loyalty said already knowing who Mike was from the street. They both looked to the door when they heard a knock. Laurel opened it smiling and reached over to Mike. "What's up baby sis?" Mike said pulling her in a hug and kissing the top of her head. "Hey Mikey. I've missed you." Laurel said hugging him tightly. "Missed you too baby girl." Mike said following her to the living room where Loyalty was sitting. "Mike, this is my boyfriend Loyalty. Loyalty, this is my brother Mike." Both of them shook hands and said hello. "You Loyal that rep uptown?" Mike asked. "Yea and you pretty boy Mike that rep Southside." Loyalty asked in return. "Heard nothing but good things." "Same for you. All about the paper. Not fooling around." "Same for you." Mike said then got serious. "I can see what kind of guy you are but I have to come here and ask what your plans are with my sister? What you gonna do when she goes off to school? Where you see this going? My sisters are my heart." "My name speaks everything about me. I love your sister. Matter of fact I'm in love with her. I ain't here to hit and quit, we ain't even go there. When she goes off to school, it will be hard but we will make it work. I'll go visit or she can come home. I'm not the cheating type so that's out the question. I see us getting married and having kids whenever she ready. But I will never rush her into doing anything she doesn't want to." Loyalty said honestly. "I like you, but don't hurt my sister. Her pain might cause you to get murked." "I don't plan on hurting her ever." he said. "Good." Mike turned and looked at Laurel. "You ready to get even more beautiful?" "Yes." Laurel said blushing. Mike had called and told her he was getting everything done for her, so she had called and told Tiara never mind since he was paying. "Let's go then." Mike said walking to the door. "Ok. See you later baby." Laurel said kissing Loyalty then walking out with Mike. Mike took Laurel to every place she needed to go to and paid for everything. All of her friend's decided to get dressed at Tiara's house since they all lived in the same neighborhood. They wanted to make their entrance outside for everyone to see. They were in Tiara's room getting dressed while laughing and talking. "So Ms. Laurel, are you going to give Loyalty some today?" Mel asked. "I don't know. We have to see how the night goes." She replied, a little unsure. They all had their dresses made and were showing so much skin. Loyalty, Moss, and Kelly waited outside with everyone else for them to come out. They all were dressed to the "T" and looked so good. "Hey brother. Looking good." Mya said to Loyalty when she walked up to them. "Thank you sis. I try." He said adjusting his cuffs. "Hey son-in- law. Looking good." Tiara's mother said to Moss. "Thanks ma. Where this girl at? Got me standing around in this dangerous hood." Moss said looking around. "Boy, they know not to do anything while I'm out here." Tiara mother's said looking around as well. Mya ran upstairs to see her sister. When she walked in the room, she couldn't help but smile brightly. "Laurel you look great." Mya said hugging her sister. She wore a tight fitting pink dress, with her sides out, a long split and cleavage showing. Her make-up was done to perfection and her updo was beautiful. "Thank you Mya." Laurel said kissing her cheek. "Ready ladies?" Melanie asked grabbing her clutch. "Yep." Tiara and Laurel said together. All three of the girls walked out of the apartment building and it seemed like the whole hood was out there. They were in awe of the girls. Everyone's family was taking pictures. Mike took so many pictures of Laurel as she stood with her friends. Loyalty walked over to her and kissed her lips. "You look fucking amazing." "Thank you baby. You look so handsome." Laurel said admiring him in his suit. "I try." Loyalty said posing with her. Camera's were flashing at them from every angle. After a good twenty minutes of taking pictures, they went and got in their limo to head to prom. Even though Liz called herself giving Laurel tough love, she was looking out the window at her daughter go off to prom. "You look beautiful baby girl." Liz said to herself. She wiped her tears that fell from her eyes as she watched Laurel and her friends get in the car and pull off. When they got to the prom, they were tipsy and high after chugging and smoking in the car. Pulling into the venue, the girls saw that all their classmates were heading in. When they walked inside, the music was bumping and the dance floor was crowded. The girls grabbed their guys and made their way to the middle of the party. They were having fun dancing and just enjoying the atmosphere. "It's time to announce prom king and queen. Can I have all the nominees up here?" The Principal said from the stage. Tiara was nominated for prom queen, along with a girl that all the girls didn't like named was Bianca. Bianca thought she was the shit, so Tiara was ready to beat her for the title of prom queen. She and Tiara had been having a rival against each other since they started high school. "Tiara, get ready to lose." Bianca said smiling and talking to her on the side. "Bitch please." Tiara said rolling her eyes at her but maintaining her smile. The tension between the both of them was thick and everyone knew about their rival. "You got this Tee." Mel yelled from the front. "Bitch please, it's all you B." One of Bianca friends yelled. "Bitch don't get fucked up." Mel said to her turning to her. "Mel go ahead with the tough shit. You don't want it." The girl replied stepping her way. "Please don't do it to yourself." Mel said ready to take off her earrings. "Calm down Mel." Laurel said trying to get her friend to pay attention to the moment. "Yea listen to your protector." The girl said smirking. "Yo for real Diamond just shut the fuck up, before you piss me off. You already know how I rock." Laurel said to the girl. The girl got quiet immediately. Laurel might have been a book worm and kept to herself, but she was known for whipping bitches asses. Her hands could do all the talking for her. "Damn baby I ain't know you was like that." Loyalty said once he witnessed how the girl that was talking shut up. "They know I don't play." "Ok ladies and gentlemen. The prom queen issss......." The

Principal said dragging it out. "TIARA!!!!" The crowd started clapping and hollering for her. Tiara smiled and started twerking on the stage when she won. When she received her crown and sash, she took the mic to make her speech. "I would like to thank all my folks who voted for me and y'all that didn't. Bianca this win is for you. End this year with a bang and you still and will always be second best. Shout out to my besties from another testie, Mel and Laurel. I love y'all. Shout out to my boss boyfriend too. I won, so you might be getting some tonight." Tiara said laughing causing the principal's eyes to get big when she said the last part. "That is enough Ms. Wells." The principal said going to snatch the microphone from her. "Dang Mr. Sanders you not letting me shine. It's cool though, got my message through." He looked at her and opened the other envelope. "And the winner for Prom King isssssssssssss.......Andrew." Andrew was actually Tiara's ex and the captain of the basketball and track team. When Tiara heard his name she rolled her eyes. "I would like to thank everyone who voted for me, I appreciate it. I would also like to let my queen know I still love you boo. It's me and you forever." Andrew said looking at Tiara. "Whatever." Tiara said rolling her eyes at him. Andrew laughed and smiled at her. He had cheated on her and when she found out, she fucked the girl and him up. After that he had been trying to get her back but Tiara wasn't having it. "Now the prom king and queen will have their dance." The principal said into the mic, smiling over at them. "I will pass Mr. Sanders." Tiara said getting ready to walk off stage. "You have to." Andrew said about to grab for her. "I don't have to do shit." "Kids play nice and just do the dance." Mr. Sanders pleaded. They both went to the middle of the floor. A slow song started to play. Andrew grabbed Tiara around the waist, pulling her in and started to dance. Moss was pissed off but didn't want to cause a scene. "You know I miss you Tiara." Andrew whispered in her ear. "I don't want to hear it Andrew." She said, trying to lean away from him. "Why are you here with that nigga?" "He is my boyfriend. Now this dance is over." Tiara said trying to pull away from him but he held her tighter. "He can't love you like I can." Andrew said pulling her closer to him. She tried to get out of his grip again. "No he loves me better." Moss saw her struggling and walked on the dance floor like he owned it. Talking to Andrew calmly, he said, "My man. I think you should let my girl go." Andrew laughed at him then said "This is my girl." "Ex, nigga get it correct." Tiara said still trying to get out of his grip. "Shut the fuck up Tiara. Ain't nobody talking to you." Andrew said turning to her. Moss swung on Andrew and connected with his jaw, knocking him out cold. "Nigga don't you ever and I mean ever in your life disrespect my girl. Nigga lost his mind." Moss said heated. "Come on baby." Tiara said pulling Moss but he wasn't moving. He wanted to murder Andrew but he knew he couldn't do it right here with so many people. He allowed Tiara to pull him away but not before taking a mental picture of how Andrew looked. "I think it's time for us to leave." Kelly said laughing. "Why?" Mel asked, not wanting to cut her partying short. "First ,my nigga just knocked the prom king out, then your ass about to fight some bitch, and Laurel ass just got bitches shutting up off break." Kelly said laughing. "Naw, we gonna let them enjoy their prom. If they want to put us out then they can come and tell us." Loyalty said walking to the dance floor with Laurel. The rest of the night went smoothly. Andrew got off the floor. Too embarrassed from getting knocked out, he left early. When prom was over, they decided to go get food. "Y'all going to the after party?" Brandy, their mutual friend asked. "I don't feel like it." Laurel said yawning. "We might stop by." Tiara said holding on to Moss' hand. "I'm down for it." Mel said still ready to party. "Cool." Brandy said heading out. After they ate their I-Hop. They all decided to go to the after party. Even though Laurel didn't want to go, she knew she couldn't let her girls go by themselves. Knowing how much beef they had with other girls, she wasn't gonna let them step into any traps. Pulling up at the party, they saw it was popping. There were drinks, weed and everything all over the place. People were dancing, having sex and some were passed out. "Yo this party wild as shit." Kelly said looking around in amazement. "Let's dance daddy." Mel said pulling on his hand. Mel led Kelly to the dance floor where she started grinding on him. Tiara and Moss were in their own zone puffing on a blunt that he had rolled. "Let's go get some drinks." Laurel said looking up at Loyalty. They were taking shots of white, drinking from their solo cups and enjoying themselves. "OHHHHHHHHHH yea we got them Hottie girls in here." The DJ yelled, talking about Bianca and her crew. They started to make noise. "But I'm looking for them Pretty Gurlsssss." The DJ said talking about Laurel, Tiara, Mel. Laurel started to make noise and Loyalty looked at her. "You in a group?" Loyalty said wide eyed. "They gave us that nickname at school." Laurel said laughing at his expression. Somewhere in the crowd, they heard... "Fuck them pretty gurls." Laurel scanned the party looking for Tiara and Mel. She didn't see Tiara, but she saw Mel in Diamond's face. "Baby it's about to go down. You might want to find Kelly and Moss." Laurel said pushing her way through the party to get to where Mel was. "What's all that shit you was talking earlier Mel?" Diamond said in her face. "Bitch I ain't about that talking shit." Mel said. "My hands act accordingly." Diamond swung and stole the shit out of Mel. She recovered fast and went to work on Diamond. She was beating the shit out of Diamond when Bianca and the other girls jumped in it. Laurel finally made it and started throwing punches off break. Moss and Tiara just came back to the party after getting a quickie in when they ran into Loyalty. "What's going on? It looks like a big ass fight over there." Moss said looking over to where the crowd was huddled. Loyalty turned around and said "Oh shit Laurel went that way to get Mel." As soon as that left Loyalty's mouth, Tiara took off running. She wasted no time fighting the other girls when she made it through. Kelly walked out the bathroom and saw his friends heading to the big crowd that looked like a fight. "Who fighting?" Kelly asked. "I think our girls, but let me be sure before I shut this party down." Loyalty said walking through the people. When they got close up, they saw their girlfriends fucking up at least seven girls between them. Moss, Loyalty and Kelly wasted no time pulling them out the crowd. "Naw bae, put me down. That bitch hit me." Mel said trying to get out of

Kelly's arms. "Calm down. You already beat her ass." Kelly said pulling her out the party. After the fight, all of them got in their separate cars and left. Loyalty and Laurel didn't say anything the whole ride. They both were in their own thoughts. When they got in the house, Laurel went straight to the bathroom to take a shower, while Loyalty sat on the couch watching TV. Laurel came from out of the shower and dressed in one of Loyalty's shirts. He looked up from the TV when he heard her come into the living room. "Why you just standing there baby?" Loyalty asked when she didn't come further in. "I want to say sorry for tonight." She said, playing with the hem of the t-shirt. "What you apologizing for?" "For fighting and stuff. That's a side of me I never want you to see." Laurel said fiddling with her fingers and looking down. "Come here baby." he patted the seat next to him. Laurel walked over to him and sat down, still not looking at the ground. Loyalty grabbed her chin and said "Baby you didn't do anything wrong. We gonna be together forever so I need to know all sides of you just like you need to know all sides of me." "I thought us fighting might ruin your night." "Nope it didn't. At least I know my baby can fight." Loyalty smiled. Loyalty and Laurel were looking into each other's eyes when Laurel leaned in and kissed his lips. Deepening the kiss, she climbed onto his lap and started unbuttoning his shirt. Holding her by the ass, he took control of the kiss. Finally getting his shirt off, she could feel his hard dick right under her. She started to grind on his erection while he gripped her ass tighter. "Fuck Laurel." Loyalty said with his lips still pressed against hers. He pulled her shirt over her head and revealed her naked body. Licking his lips, he admired her from her pert breasts, to her full hips, to her clean shaven pussy. "Make love to me Loyalty." Laurel said reaching for his belt buckle. Stopping her hands, he looked at her. "You sure about this baby?" He asked. He wanted to make sure she was ready. Moaning and rocking back and forth on his dick, she replied, "Yes." Loyalty kissed her passionately, moving down to her neck sucking on it, causing moans to escape her mouth. He laid her on the couch with ease, then sucked on her breast, taking turns sucking and massaging each breast. Laurel was so wet that every touch from him caused her to moan. He kissed down from her breasts to her and stomach and further. Reaching her pussy, he gave her clit a flick, causing her to moan louder. Spreading her lips, he stuck his tongue inside of her. Laurel was squirming from the movement of his tongue so deep inside of her. Loyalty locked his arm around her legs so she wouldn't run away from him. While he tongue fucked her, he used his finger and played with her clit, applying pressure and rubbing in circles. Laurel was going crazy. Her body was reaching an orgasm that had her screaming, moaning and calling Loyalty's name all together. She felt her body heat up and before she knew it, she came so long and hard, she started to shake. Wiping his mouth, Loyalty got up and looked at her. "That was good." Loyalty said biting on his bottom lip while looking at her naked body. The things he planned on doing to her made his dick even harder. He picked her up and took her to the room. Wanting her first time to be comfortable he placed her in the middle of the bed and went to turn on a slow mix. When he dropped his pants, Laurel's eyes got big. She saw him naked before and even touched his dick, but for some reason, it looked extra-long and thick tonight. She took a deep breath, trying to prepare herself. Loyalty grabbed a gold pack from his bedside drawer and positioned himself over her. "Are you ready?" "Yes." Laurel said nervously. Her body was wound up tight with nerves. She didn't know what to expect or how painful it would be. He placed himself at her entrance and watched as her chest rose up and down. He eased himself inside of her and she instantly tensed up. "Baby relax or it's going to hurt more." Loyalty said kissing her face. While kissing her, he eased in more. Laurel let out a grunt as she felt her muscles expanding to take him in. "Owwwwww." Laurel said as he pushed in further. She reached for the sheets below her and scrunched them in her hands. "Do you want me to stop?" Loyalty asked looking down at her in the push up position. "No, keep going." she said taking deep breaths. Loyalty knew since she was a virgin, he would have to go easy to loosen it up. He inched in more and more till he was inside of her to the hilt. He stayed still, not moving because she was so tight. If he moved, he was going to bust and the night would be ruined. When he calmed down, he pulled out and pushed back in. He felt Laurel loosening up some. Taking her leg and placing it over his hip, he started stroking her faster. Laurel started moaning louder and reached up to grab onto his arms. "I fucking love you." Loyalty said while leaning down and kissing her. Laurel started to get into it more and was fucking him back. Not wanting to cum yet, he turned her over and made her get on her hands and knees. "Throw it back on daddy." Loyalty said as smacked her ass. Pushing his dick back inside her, he watched as Laurel started throwing her ass back to him. Grabbing her air and squeezing her waist, he rotated his hips, hitting her G-spot repeatedly. Laurel felt her orgasm near. She didn't have any warning when he hit a sensitive spot inside her. She screamed his name "Loyalllllltttyyyyyyyyyyy." As her orgasm hit hard, her muscles pulled him deeper inside of her. Feeling her squeeze him tight, he pulled her up, making her back meet his chest, "Fuck Laurel baby, I'm about to cum. You feel so fucking good." Grabbing his arm, Laurel felt him push in hard on his last thrust as he came. She fell face first into the pillows, while Loyalty fell to her side. "Damn. I'm glad I met you when I did. I can't imagine being without you." Running his fingers down her spine, he leaned over and placed a kiss to her forehead. Laurel turned on her side to face him. "I love you babe. I'm glad I waited and saved myself for you." "I love you too. Now let's go take a shower and clean up." After Loyalty washed Laurel and himself, they both went back to bed and fell asleep with his arms securely around her.

Chapter 20

MYA

Mya was relaxing in her room and texting on her cell phone when she heard her door open. She looked up to see her mother. "Hey ma, what's up?" Mya asked. "Why is your ass still in the bed?" Liz asked, leaning on the doorframe. "Ma, it's Saturday and it's 9 o'clock in the morning." Mya said looking at her mother like she was crazy. "You won't be going outside today. You cleaning the whole house up." "Why I have to clean the whole house up?" she asked sitting up. "If you don't like it you can leave too." Mya just looked at her mother, not saying a word. She knew if she didn't get up, her mother would bitch all day, so she got up out of the bed and started to clean the house. As soon as she was done, all she wanted to do was sleep but she knew if Liz was home that would be impossible. "Mya, come here." Liz yelled. Mya walked to the kitchen to see what her mother wanted. "Yes ma." "Did you use bleach on the mop?" Liz asked. "No I used pine sol." Next thing Mya knew her mother smacked the shit out of her. "I swear you don't listen. I said use bleach." She yelled. Mya held her face looking at her mother. Her mother had to be going off the deep end. "Now mop this shit over." Liz said walking out of the kitchen. Mya wanted to cry so badly but didn't want to give her mother the satisfaction of seeing her hurt. She was in the finishing process of mopping, when she heard a knock on the door. "Who is it?" Mya asked walking to the front. "It's me." Laurel said. Mya opened the door fast. She was so happy to see her sister. "Laurel I miss you." Mya said hugging her tight. "Dang girl. I have only been gone for a week." Laurel said hugging her sister back. "Well a week is long enough." She whispered. "You can always come over whenever you want to." Laurel said looking at her. "Cool! So what brings you over?" Mya asked. She didn't want her sister to even leave now. "I came to give you the ticket for my graduation and my prom picture." Laurel said handing them to Mya from her bag. "Dang Laurel you look good." Mya said looking at the prom picture of her and Loyalty. "What the hell is she doing here?" Liz asked coming out her room and seeing Laurel sitting on the couch with Mya. "Don't worry, I was just leaving. See you later Mya. I love you." Laurel stood up walking towards the door. "I love you too Laurel. I'll see you Monday." She said, almost breaking down in tears. Laurel looked at her, smiled and walked out the door. "I don't want her in my damn house." Liz yelled to Mya. Mya just rolled her eyes. She was getting tired of being under Liz's reign of terror. For the whole weekend, Mya was stuck in the house with her mother. Monday morning, Mya got up and got dressed, ready to head to her sister's graduation. "Where the hell you think you going?" Liz asked sitting at the table drinking her coffee. "I'm going to Laurel's graduation. They are on their way to pick me up." Mya said. "Did you ask me if you can go?" Liz asked sipping her coffee. "I thought I could go. It is my sister's graduation." She said shrugging her shoulders. "You ain't going anywhere." Liz said placing her mug down and looking up at her. "And if I do?" Mya questioned her mother crossing her arms over her chest. "I will beat your ass and make sure you never step foot back into this house." Liz said raising her eyebrow, giving her the "try me if you want" look. Mya looked at her mother and grabbed her purse and headed to the door. When went to open the door, Liz pulled her by her hair and started to whip her like a girl off the street. Mya cried and screamed for Liz to stop but she didn't. As soon as Liz took a break, Mya took that chance and ran out the door. When she got outside, she was crying so bad and in so much pain. She sat on the front step with her head in her lap. "Mya." Laurel called from Loyalty's car when they pulled up. Mya was crying so bad she didn't hear her. "Baby I think something's wrong with her." Laurel said getting out the car to check on her sister. "Mya baby what's wrong?" Laurel said sitting next to her. Mya looked up and Laurel's saw her face. "What the fuck happened?" Laurel asked taking in her disheveled hair and busted lip. "Our mother is what happened. She beat me because I wanted to go to your graduation and told me don't come back." Mya said as tears fell from her face. "I'm so sorry Mya." She said hugging her sister. "Come on. I'll take you to the hospital to make sure nothing is broke." Laurel said walking her to the car. "Nooooo." Mya yelled then looked at her "We going to your graduation. You worked too hard to not be on that stage giving your speech. I will put shades on or something." "Are you sure?" Laurel asked still looking her over. She face was starting to swell a little. "I'm sure." They got in the car and Loyalty looked at Mya. "What happened lil sis?" Loyalty asked getting pissed. "Please don't ask." Mya said trying to fix her face. "Oh baby, Mya's going to have to live with us. Well until I leave, then we can figure something out." Laurel said looking at him. "Ok." Loyalty said grabbing her hand and kissing it. Since they were running late, Laurel jumped out the car and ran in while they parked. "So lil sis, you going to tell me what happened?" Loyalty asked while they walked to the stadium. "I rather just wait to tell you when I tell Mike because I know as soon as he sees me he going to ask the same thing." Mya said, her arms crossed over her chest. Loyalty left it alone and headed to the seat where Mike was at. "What's good Loyalty and baby sis?" Mike said then looked at Mya again. "What the fuck happened to your face?" Mike asked turning red. "Mike I will tell you later but please stay clam so we can focus on Laurel." She said, trying to keep him from lashing out. Mike let it go for now and focused his attention to the front. "Now let me introduce our valedictorian. This young lady excels in every class, has a GPA of 4.80 and is also a member of the dance team. She will be attending Harvard University in the fall. Please welcome this year's valedictorian, Laurel Adams." The principal announced. Everyone cheered as Laurel got up to the stage. "Good morning everyone. I would first like to say congratulations to the class of 2003. We made it. I would like to say that high school was the opening door to what our future will lead us too. Some of us had it easy, some had it hard, but no matter how we got to this day, we overcame each and every obstacle that we came in contact with. We had people to support us and have our backs to the end. As we walk across this stage we dedicate these diplomas and futures to them. I know for me, it might look like it was easy but I worked hard and made sure I gave my loved ones something to be proud of. I would like to dedicate this diploma and my future success to my big brother Mike, my little sister Mya, my best friends Tiara and Mel, my wonderful boyfriend Loyalty and last but not least my parents. They might not be here but I have to thank them for showing me how to never give up and work for my success. Once again, congratulations class of 2003." Laurel said ending her speech with a lot of cheers. As they called names to walk across the stage, Mike managed to get to the front to take some pictures, and also record her. After they were done, they went outside and took pictures and headed to Ruth Chris Steakhouse for dinner. Mike hugged his sister tight. "I'm so proud of you Laurel. You did it." "Thank you Mikey." Laurel said smiling at her big brother. He handed her a gift bag "Here go your graduation gift." Laurel took the paper out and was shocked to see a Gucci book bag and a mac laptop. "Oh my goodness Mike. Thank you so much." Laurel said jumping to hug him. "I couldn't send you off to Harvard without being in style." Mike said kissing the top of her head. "Here is my gift Laurel. It's not much but it's something." Mya said handing her the gift. Laurel opened it and tears weld up in her eyes. It was a picture of the two of them when Mya was three and Laurel was six. She was teaching Mya how to ride a bike. The frame said world's best sister. "Mya I love it." Laurel said reaching over and hugging her tight. "Here's your gift baby." Loyalty said passing her a big box. She opened it and saw a beautiful bracelet, necklace and earrings. "These are beautiful. Thank you babe." Laurel said, leaning over and kissing him. They ate and talked for a little then Loyalty said "Oh I almost forgot about your last gift." "I don't need anything else." Laurel said still in awe of what she got. "This is actually from me and your brother." Loyalty said handing her a clue card. "A card with a clue on it?" Laurel looked at both of them. "Mya can help you out." Mike said. "Since you have me, no longer will you have to pay $1.10 each way." Laurel read out loud. "Oh my goodness. You got a car Laurel." Mya said with excitement. "What? Oh my goodnessssss...y'all brought me a car?" Laurel asked shocked. Loyalty gave her the keys to a brand new BMW. "OMG thank y'all." Laurel said hugging everyone. To say this was the best day was an understatement. She was beyond happy to be surrounded by the people she loved most. After the excitement wore down, Mike looked over to Mya. "Mya what happened to you?" he asked in a low voice. "Ma did this to me this morning." Mya said looking down at the table. "What?" Mike yelled. "Ma beat me for wanting to go to Laurel's graduation and also put me out." "Yo I'm really going to talk to ma. That shit is uncalled for." Mike said mad as fuck. "Mike just please leave it alone. If she wants to feel like she doesn't have any children, then we will let her be miserable by herself." Laurel said, tired of her mother's attitude. "You right Laurel. We are not going to ruin your day." Mike said, still mad. After dinner Mya, Laurel and Loyalty headed home. "Rules for my house Mya, so we all can be on the same page." Loyalty said once they got comfortable on the couch. "You like my lil sister so I'm not going to try and be your father. So all I'm asking is that you respect me and your sister place. Do not have that nigga in my house because I don't fuck with him." Loyalty said looking at her. "The girls can come over and you can have company just let me and Laurel know. Do you understand?" "Yes I understand." Mya said nodding. "Cool, glad we on the same page." he said then looked at his ringing phone and picked it up. "You ok Mya?" Laurel asked her sister. "Yea I'm good. I was just thinking about mommy." Mya said laying on her sister's lap while she played in her hair. "Yea, she will realize she just lost some really cool kids." Laurel said with a chuckle. "Laurel, how are you so strong with everything going on?" "Want to know a secret?" "Yea." "I'm not that strong. I break down and have my low points but I have Loyalty to pick me up and realize my worth. Having someone in your corner helps and I will always be in yours." "You really in love, huh?" Smiling, she looked down at her sister. "Yea I am. He makes me happy." "I want love like that one day." Mya sighed. "You will have it one day Mya." Loyalty walked out of the room with all black on. "Aye baby, I have some business to handle. I will be home late at night so don't stay up. I'll call you. You know how it is." Loyalty said. "Yeah I know. Be safe please." Laurel said giving him a kiss. "Always baby. I love you." "I love you too." "See you later big head." Loyalty said to Mya shaking her head that was still in Laurel's lap. "Later brother."

Chapter 21

3 MONTHS LATER

"Laurel is this everything you taking with you?" Loyalty asked grabbing her bags so she can head to school. "Yea, since the apartment is furnished I don't need anything." She said. "Well let's get on the road before it's too late." Loyalty told her. He was driving with her to school and was going to fly back. "Ok. Mya please behave yourself. Loyalty will be back on Sunday. Do you think you can stay out of trouble for a week?" Laurel asked her sister because she knew how Mya could be. "Of course Laurel. I'm going to miss you." Mya said hugging her sister. "I'm going to miss you too. I love you." Laurel said on the verge of tears. "I love you too sis." "Yo Mya remember my rule." Loyalty said pointing his finger at her. "I know I know." Mya said rolling her eyes. "Where is Mikey. I need to tell him I love him before I leave?" Laurel said. She already told her best friends she will see them later and that they can visit her. Melanie and Tiara decided to go to college locally. There was a knock on the door

165

and Laurel went to open it, seeing Mike standing on the other side. "I made it just in time huh?" He said pulling her in a tight hug. "Yes. I love you Mike." Laurel said holding on to her big brother. "Show them white kids that black girls are 10 times smarter than them." "I will." She laughed. Mike kissed her forehead and let her go. "If you need anything please call me." Mike said knowing how Laurel could be. She never asked for anything, wanting to be independent. "Ok." "Alright y'all. We have to hit the road." Loyalty said grabbing the last of her bags, heading to the door. Laurel looked at her brother and sister and smiled. Little did she know, both of their lives was about to be turned upside down once she started school. Mya... Mya was in the house watching TV when her cell phone rang. Looking at the screen, she saw that Kyle was calling. "Hello." She answered on the 2nd ring. "What you doing?" Kyle asked. "Nothing, just watching TV. What you doing?" "Just finished making money. I'm about to come through." Kyle had been selling drugs and making a good amount of money off it. Kyle knew that she lived with Loyalty and dropped her off a few times at the house. "I don't know if that's a good idea." Mya said. "Damn, so you don't want to spend time with your man or something?" Kyle asked, trying to get her to say yes. "No, it's not like that. I would love to spend time with you, but this is Loyalty's house and he said no company over." "So you are taking orders from another nigga. Damn are you fucking him or something?" Kyle asked pissed off. "No I'm not fucking him. Ok Kyle if you want to come over you can." Mya said not wanting to anger him anymore. "I will be there in 20 minutes. You gonna cook for a nigga?" Kyle asked licking his lips. "I can cook for you if you want." "Good." Kyle said hanging up without saying good-bye. Mya was so happy it was just Friday and Loyalty wouldn't be home until Sunday. She went in the kitchen and decided fry some chicken and make rice with greens. She was cooking when her phone started to ring. "Hello." "What's the apartment number?" "405"Mya said. Kyle didn't even reply. He just hung up. 5 minutes later Mya heard a knock at the door. "Who is it?" "Open the damn door." Mya opened the door and Kyle stood there looking good. He had a fresh haircut, his goatee was neatly trimmed and he had a fresh outfit out. He gave Mya a slow smile. "What's up beautiful?" he said. "Nothing. Your dinner is ready." He pulled her into him and kissed her deep. "That's a good wife. Cooking for your man." Kyle said causing Mya to blush. She made their plates and they sat on the couch eating while watching a movie. As soon as they were done eating, Kyle wasted no time pulling his pants down. Mya knew he wanted head. Even though she didn't want to give it to him, she knew not to piss him off. She sucked his dick until he came in her mouth. Swallowing all of his seeds, he pulled her up and made her straddle his lap with her legs on either side of him. Since she had on a large tee shirt and underclothes, he moved her panties to the side and entered her forcefully. "Ahhhh." Mya yelled as Kyle entered her. She wasn't wet enough, so when he pushed inside her, it started to sting. "Ride me." He said, smacking her ass. Mya started to rock back and forth on Kyle not sure if she was doing it right. Kyle normally just fucked her the way he wanted and never let her have any control. She wasn't sure if she was doing it right or not, but she was trying. "Slim, what the fuck you doing? Ride me. Mya shit." Kyle said grabbing her ass tightly, causing a little pain . "I'm trying Ky, let go." She said bouncing up and down on his dick. "Smack, smack", he repeatedly smacked her ass, leaving hand prints. "Fuck this. Your ass can't do shit right. Get up and bend over." Mya did as she was told and bent over the couch. Without warning, he forced his dick inside of her. Pulling her panties further to the side to gain more access, he showed no mercy on her pussy. With a tight grip on her waist, he pounded into her harder and harder. Mya moans, mixed with cries could be heard all through the house. "Now can you at least throw that shit back now?" Kyle asked going deeper inside of her. Mya started to throw it back harder on Kyle. Each stroke he gave her, she returned with a powerful thrust back to him. Two minutes later, Kyle was coming inside of Mya. Out of breath he pulled out and sat on the couch, watching Mya fix her panties. "When that nigga supposed to come back?" Kyle asked after she finally fixed herself up. "Sunday. Why?" "I'm spending the night, that's why." He said lighting a blunt. "Ok." "Yo I don't want you staying here anymore. I'm getting my own place in two weeks. You moving in with me." Kyle said passing her the blunt. "My brother or sister won't allow me to move in with you." Mya said hitting the blunt. "Fuck what they say. Are you going to keep letting people step between our love?" Mya looked at Kyle and saw the spark of anger in his eyes. It made her nervous to answer him. "No." "Sometimes I feel like you don't love me." "I do love you Kyle you know that." "You need to start proving it." Kyle said focusing back on the movie and finishing up his blunt. Mya didn't say anything else. So much was going through her head and she didn't know what to do. "Are you ready to go to bed?" Mya asked getting sleepy. "Yea, which one is your room?" Mya lead him to her room. Walking in the room Kyle only said one word "Strip." No hesitation at all, Mya took off her oversized shirt and her underclothes, waiting for the next instructions. "Now get on the bed." Mya did what she was told. "Open your legs wide." Kyle smiled when he saw her wet pussy with his cum still smeared around it. "Play with your clit." "What?" Mya said looking at him nervously. She never played with herself before and he never asked her to do anything like that. "Just do it." Kyle said sternly. Taking a deep breath, Mya started to rub her clit. At first it wasn't doing anything for her, so she started pressing down on it while rotating her fingers. After awhile it started to feel good to her. She was wondering why she never did this before. Getting lost in the moment of getting to know herself better, she felt herself about to cum. Kyle watched her with a smirk on his face while he jerked his dick getting himself harder. Mya had her head back, eyes closed, loving the feeling of her fingers. Kyle couldn't take it anymore and without warning, rammed his dick inside of her causing a loud scream to escape and her eyes to fly open. "This shit feels good baby." Kyle said humping the shit out of her. Mya started to fuck him back as he gave her deep, long strokes. "Fuck, I'm about to cum." Kyle said pulling out and cumming on her stomach. "Damn. Go take a shower and come back to bed." Kyle said laying down. Mya didn't say anything.

She got up and went to the bathroom that was connected to her room. As soon Mya went to the shower, Kyle picked his phone up. "What do you want LaKeisha?" "I have been calling you all day?" "And your point is?" "You must be with her? That's the only time you be treating me like that." "Look, I'm with my woman, so don't call me. I'll call you." Kyle said hanging up on her. He got up and went in the shower with Mya. "What you doing in here?" Mya asked looking at Kyle in surprise. Kyle shut her up with a kiss and bent her over, not caring that he just got her hair wet. He fucked her in the shower, getting himself another quick nut. They both washed up and headed to bed to finally get some sleep. The next morning Mya was so sore from the rough sex that Kyle gave her, but she was happy to wake up next to him. She made him breakfast and they both were sitting on the couch watching TV when they heard the front door open. Mya froze, and Kyle had a smirk on his face like he owned the place. "Yeah baby I'm just walking in. I'll call you later." Loyalty said on the phone. Loyalty hung up the phone and looked in his living room and saw Kyle and Mya sitting on his couch. "Mya please tell me I'm fucking dreaming." Loyalty said grilling the shit out of Kyle. "Um, Loyalty he just came over to drop something off." Mya said quickly. "Mya I gave you one rule. I'm going to go to my room and when I come back out please let that nigga be out of my house, or he getting smoked." Loyalty said pissed off. Mya looked at Kyle and let him know he had to go. Kyle laughed and kissed Mya saying, "Call me in a little." Loyalty walked back out of his room and looked at Mya. "Really Mya?" "I'm sorry. We were just watching

TV." "But I asked you to not have him in my house. How can I trust you if I leave for a week and you have that nigga in my house? I'm about to call your sister and it's going to be her call." Loyalty said pulling his phone out and dialing Laurel's number. She answered quickly. "Hello." Laurel said on speaker. "So I come home and Mya has that nigga in my house. It's your call, because right now I'm pissed off." Loyalty said rubbing his wavy hair "Mya, why would you have him in the house?" Laurel yelled. "We were just watching TV." Mya said on the verge of tears. She knew she fucked up. "That's not the point. Look school starts Monday. I think it's best if you move with Mike. I don't want Loyalty to feel like he can't leave and handle business because you gonna have that boy in his house." Laurel said sighing. "Fine. I will go pack my stuff." Mya said walking to her room, done with the conversation. Mya was packing her stuff when Mike arrived to pick her up. She just looked at Loyalty not saying anything to him. She was mad at him. She felt like he was overreacting and then to call her sister was stretching it.

Chapter 22

SOPHOMORE YEAR (2004)

——◦◦》》⊗◦》⊗⊗◦《《◦◦——

School had started and surprisingly Mya and Mike living together was going good. She was still upset with Laurel and Loyalty. She felt like they betrayed her. Mike's only rules were to not fuck in his house and go to school. If she did that he was cool, plus he stayed out all night hustling so he was hardly home. The down fall of living with Mike was his new girlfriend Amber. Amber was an uptight, gold digger who couldn't stand Mya or Laurel. Mya was walking down the hall of school, bored out of her mind. "Yo Mya. Why you in the hall?" Tamara asked catching up with her as she walked from the batroom. "I'm bored. I'm thinking about going home. What you doing in the hall?" "Just came from the bathroom." Tamara said then looked at Mya and asked "Have you talked to Laurel?" "Naw, why?" "The other day when she talked to Tiara, she asked how you doing and stuff. Shoot she always ask how you doing." Tamara said. "Well she know how I'm doing. I'm sure cause she talks to Mike." She said looking at her phone and saw a text from Kyle telling her he was outside. "Check it Tamara. I'll catch you and the girls later. I'm out." Not waiting for a response, she walked out the school and got in Kyle's car that was parked out front. Getting in, she leaned over the arm rest and gave him a kiss. "We going to my house." Kyle said heading to his new apartment that was in a crack head's name along with his car. Without even saying anything, as soon as they walked in the apartment, Mya took all her clothes off and got on her knees, giving him head. He was so happy that he turned her out. He didn't even have to tell her what he wanted anymore, she just did it. Sitting on the couch he enjoyed himself by smoking a blunt and watching his dick disappear in Mya's mouth. She was so focused on her task that she didn't hear her phone ring until Kyle answered it. "Hello." Kyle said exhaling the smoke. "Yo let me speak to Mya." Lord said, not caring that Kyle answered her phone. "Man didn't I tell you to stop calling my girl. She busy right now. Keep calling her and your ass won't ever play basketball again." Kyle said getting angry. "Nigga whatever. Tell her to call me when she finished being busy." Lord said hanging up. Kyle was pissed now. Unaware that he had answered her phone, he pulled Mya up by her hair. "Ouch Kyle." Mya said looking at him and trying to grab her hair from his hand. "What I tell you about that nigga Lord calling you?" Kyle said looking at her. "He is just my best friend." "You don't need any male best friends. I'm your best friend. Tell that nigga to stop calling you." Kyle said tightening his grip on her hair. "Okkkkk." Mya said trying to loosen up his grip. Loosening his grip on her hair, he looked at her with so much disgust and said "I'm not in the mood anymore. Get dressed and get your shit so I can take you home." "Baby I will tell him, don't be mad." She hated when he was mad at her. "You keep saying that shit but he keep fucking calling. You are being a shitty ass girlfriend right now." Mya grabbed her phone quickly and called Lord back. "Yo, that clown nigga answered your phone faking." Lord said with a chuckle when he answered. "Lord, we can't be friends anymore. It's causing problems in my relationship." Mya said about to cry. Lord laughed then added "Cool Slim." Mya hung up and looked at Kyle, who had a smirk on his face, then pulled her to him. "I love you baby." Kyle said kissing her. "I love you too." Mya got on top on him and rode him, as he roughly grabbed her breast and sucked on her neck. Being the selfish nigga he is, he came and pulled out of Mya, drained. Around 5pm, Kyle had to make some runs so he took Mya home. She put her key in the door and saw Amber and her friends sitting on the couch. Rolling her eyes she went to her room. "I can't stand that little bitch." Amber said to her friends. Mya heard her but didn't say anything. "Hello." Mya said answering her ringing phone. It was Destiny calling. "Where were you after school? I was looking for you. Lord was having a game and wanted all of us to come." Destiny said with a lot of noise in the background. "I was with Kyle and where are you? It's noisy." "It's a block party. You should come through." Destiny said. Mya informed Destiny she was on her way and headed to the block party. Arriving shortly after, she noticed that everyone was outside. She walked over to her friends and noticed that Scott and Lord were with them. "What's up sis?" Scott said hugging her. "Nothing." Mya said then looked at Lord. "Lord, can I talk to you for a second?" Mya asked nervously. "Now you want to talk to me?" Lord said mugging her. "I'm sorry. What you want me to do?" "Stick up for yourself. Stop letting that nigga control your life. Boyfriend or not, I'm your best friend. You dissing me over a nigga that is controlling you and shit." Looking up at him, she gave him the puppy dog eyes. "I'm sorry. Please forgive me." "You lucky I love your lil ass." Lord said giving her a hug then looked at her and said "If that nigga come at me wrong again, I'm fucking him up." "Ok I will keep y'all two away from each other." Mya said laughing. "There go your real boyfriend." Lord said. Mya turned around and saw Shad walking towards them with Eric and Micah. "Shut up. You know me and Shad is just cool. There go your girlfriend." Mya said pointing out Keya. "Real funny. I told you I'm not ready for a good girl yet." Lord said smirking. Mya and her friends were having fun when Mike walked up. "Hey Mikeeeee." Destiny said smiling at him. "Hey Destiny." Mike said then looked at Mya and said "I'm going out of town tonight so Amber is going to look after you." "Um Mike, Amber don't like me, so how about I stay at Destiny's house." "Your call baby. Just let me know." Mike said. "I'm going to stay with Destiny." "Cool. I'll be home tomorrow." Mike said giving her some money. The block party was coming to an end and everyone was starting to head home. "I need to go get clothes. Walk with me Destiny." Mya said. "Ok. Scott and Shad said they going to walk with us." Shad walked up on the side of Mya. "So Mya how you been? I haven't seen you around as much lately." "I been fine and I know I don't be out as much as I use to." "I can tell. You still with Kyle?" Shad asked hoping she would say no. "Yeah why?" "I was just asking." He said with a deep breath. Using her key to get in the apartment, she saw Amber was still there, causing her to roll her eyes at her. "I thought you were staying at your friend's house." "I thought you had some business to mind." Destiny snapped at her. "Who the fuck you think you talking to little girl?" Amber said looking at Destiny. "Your hoe ass." she said not backing down. "Come on Dest, she not worth it. Y'all can come in. I'm just getting clothes." Mya said pulling Destiny with her. "I can't stand that hoe." she said. "Me either." Mya packed her clothes and they all headed out. For the whole weekend, she stayed with Destiny and had fun. She talked to Kyle but he was so busy, he didn't have time to see or talk to her. Sunday night, she headed back home thinking her brother was home, but was greeted by Amber's annoying ass. A week went by and she hadn't heard or seen her brother. She started to get worried. After a long day of school, she walked in the house and saw Amber in the kitchen. "Mya, have you talked to your brother?" she asked. "No, I'm starting to get worried. Have you?" "No." Mya was in her own thoughts when her phone rang. "Hello." "You have a collect call from Mike. Do you want to accept the charges?" "Yes." The phone connected to Mike. "Mike what the heck?" "I'm good, don't worry. They got me on some bull shit. I'll be home soon." Mike said trying to make sure she wasn't worried. "Mike, what am I going to do while you gone?" "Keep going to school. Let me speak to Amber." Mya passed Amber the phone.

"Baby is you Okay? Where are you?" Amber asked faked concerned. "I got locked up. They say I'm looking at 5 years, but they don't have anything. I should be home soon. Please take care of my little sister." "I will baby, I love you." "I love you too." Mya talked back to Mike and he told her Amber will be looking after her. She knew her life was about to be hell if she was under the care of Amber.

Chapter 23

YEAR LATER (2005)...

⟶ ⟫⦿⟪ ⟵

After Mike got locked up, Mya's life went downhill. Amber was trifling as fuck. Every time Mya would leave, she would have her friends in the house, niggas in the house and she was using all of Mike's stash money like it was nothing. Mya had started staying with Kyle more. She felt like she was alone. She still wasn't talking to Laurel or Loyalty. When they called her phone she would press ignore. The only thing that was going good for her is her grades in school. She was a junior now. She was in the café, when her girls sat down. "What's up girl? You look tired." Destiny said. "I am. Amber had a party at the house last night keeping me up. Kyle didn't answer his phone so I couldn't stay with him." Mya said, laying her head on the table. "Why you didn't come over my house?" Destiny asked. "Yea you could have stayed with me too?" Tamara and Britt agreed. "I didn't want to impose. Y'all mothers already doing a lot for me." "Girl you know my mother don't mind if you stay over." Destiny said. "Ours don't either." Tamara and Britt said. Before Mya could respond, her phone rang and it was Kyle. "Hello." She answered. "I'm outside. Come on." "I can't leave school right now. I have a test next period." Mya said. "Fuck that test, your man need you. So bring your ass outside now, or I'm coming in there to get you. You have 10 minutes." Kyle said then hung up on her. Mya put her head down then looked at her friends and said "Y'all I'm leaving. I'll see y'all later." "But Mya, the test next period is important. It's 15% of your grade." Destiny said looking at her like she had gone insane. "I know. Just tell them I don't feel too well." Mya said getting up and going to get her stuff. When she walked outside, Kyle and all of his boys was in the car. She rolled her eyes and walked over to the car and got in the front. "It took your ass long enough." Kyle said. Mya didn't say anything. She knew how disrespectful he can get in front of his friends. She just sat back and rode with them as they made several stops, dropping drugs off and picking up money. Mya never understood why Kyle liked for her to ride with him and his boys while they made their runs. After the last pick up they headed to Kyle's house. "Alright niggas. I'll see y'all later, I'm going to spend time with my lady." Kyle told his boys. Mya and Kyle walked in his apartment and Kyle started to kiss on her neck and put his hand in her pants. Mya wasn't really in the mood so she tried to move his hand. "What the fuck is the attitude for Mya?" "I called you all last night and you kept forwarding my calls Kyle." "I was handling fucking business. I'm fucking sorry I was busy and didn't have time to talk to my annoying ass girlfriend." "Annoying? I'm annoying now?

Fuck you Kyle." "That's what the fuck I'm trying to get you to do: fuck me. But you back on your little girl shit." "If I'm so annoying and on my little girl shit, why do you keep fucking me Kyle?" Mya asked folding her arms over her chest. "Maybe I love your dumb ass. Look, kill that fucking attitude cause you blowing my high." Kyle said lighting a blunt and sitting on the couch. Mya looked at him and rolled her eyes. Kyle didn't give a fuck about her attitude. "Here man." Kyle said throwing some keys at her while she sat on the love seat away from him. "What's this?" "Fucking house keys. I know that's why your ass was blowing up my fucking phone yesterday. You might as will move in here. Shit, all your shit is here anyways." "Whatever." Mya said rolling her eyes. "Man give my keys back if you still got that attitude. I don't want to come home to bitching every night." Mya thought about if she should give him back the key or not. She figured she would take a chance to live with him. She didn't have anyone else. "Are you going to take me to get my stuff?" "Only if you come satisfy your man." Kyle said with a smirk adjusting his hard-on. Mya got up and wasted no time giving Kyle what he wanted. When they were done, he drove her to her brother's apartment. Opening up the door she couldn't believe her eyes. It was empty. Only things that were left in there were her and Mike clothes. Mya was confused because when she left this morning it was full. "What the fuck?" Mya yelled. "Damn, where all y'all shit?" Kyle asked, walking around the empty apartment. Mya looked in the kitchen and saw a note on the counter. Mya, I couldn't play this role of a mother to a teen anymore, so I took the stuff and I'm leaving. You will be fine. Shit you have a boyfriend who is pushing, live with him and live off of him. Tell Mike I'm sorry, I love him but I can't be a tied down. I'm only 22. Amber Mya was beyond pissed off. She ran into Mike's room to his other stash. Opening up the box it was empty. All of her brother's money was gone. "That bitch." Mya said on the verge of crying. "Baby its cool. Just get your shit, you living with me now." Kyle said coming up behind her. "What I'm going to do with my brothers stuff." Kyle looked at her like she was crazy. He could give two fucks what she do with his shit. "Fuck if I know. Leave it." "I can't leave it. When he gets out, he will need something to wear." Mya said giving him a screwed up face. "We will drop it off at your mom's place then. Damn." Mya gathered hers and Mike's stuff and locked the door. When they pulled up to her neighborhood, everyone was outside; Even Lord. She was getting out the car with Mike's clothes when Destiny came over. "You moving back home?" Destiny asked grabbing one of her bags while Kyle sat in the car. He saw that she was struggling with some of the bags but he didn't make a move to help her. "No, these are Mike things. That bitch took everything and left our clothes." "What the fuck are you going to do?" Destiny asked as they rode the elevator up to the 3rd floor. "I'm moving in with Kyle." Mya said once the doors opened. Destiny stopped walking and looked at Destiny. "I don't think that's a good idea Mya." "Destiny I will be fine. Damn." Mya didn't want to hear Destiny's lecture so kept walking to her mother's apartment. Knocking on the door she waited for her mother to answer. Opening the door, Mya stood there staring at Liz. "What the fuck you want?" "Mike got locked up and his trifling girlfriend left and took everything but his clothes. I just wanted to bring them to you for when he gets out." Mya said not wanting to be in her mother's presence more than she needed to be. Liz just looked at her and said "Do it look like I want his shit at my house?" "Whatever ma." Mya said leaving his bags by her door and walking off towards the elevator. She wanted to cry so badly but didn't want to give her mother the satisfaction of seeing she got to her. Destiny opened up her arms for her best friend. "It's alright Mya." Destiny said rubbing her back. She knew her best friend was hurting behind her mother's words. "I don't know why she hates us so much?" Mya said her voice cracking. "It's ok." They both walked back out to see that all her girls and Lord was on the front. Kyle saw Lord about to say something to Mya and got out the car. He walked up to them and said "Come on baby let's go home." Grabbing Mya and pulling her to the car, he gave Lord a death stare as he pulled off. Lord... "Wait, Mya living with that nigga?" Lord asked Destiny. "Yep, Amber took all their stuff and left." "Damn, she can't stay with one of y'all? I don't trust that nigga." Lord said looking in the direction his car took off. "Is it that you don't trust him or you just love Mya?" Brittany asked smiling slightly. "I care about her safety. That nigga is no good." Lord said trying to take the attention off of him. "I understand what you saying Lord." Destiny said, still upset that Mya would decide to move in with him. "Y'all I'm out." Lord said walking to his aunt's house. When he got there, all he thought about was Mya. The first time he met her, he found her attractive and liked her, but once they started to get to know each other better, he looked at her as a little sister. The sexual attraction that was there had been replaced by a brother relationship. He would fuck Kyle up if something happened to Mya. Sitting on the couch at his aunt's house, the door opened. It was his cousin Heaven and Keya. Keya smiled at Lord but didn't say anything because she was tired of getting her feelings hurt every time she talked to him. "What you doing over her nigga?" Heaven asked. "Chilling." "Don't you have a house to chill at?" "Whatever." Lord said then looked at Keya. He admired her outfit. She looked good. He really liked her but she was just a good girl and he ain't want to turn her out or was he ready to settle down. "You not speaking today Keya?" Lord asked. "Hey Lord." Keya said then looked at Heaven "Heaven I will catch you later girl, I'm about to head home." "Ok, see you tomorrow." Keya left and Heaven turned to Lord and said "Why you always doing that to my best friend?" "Doing what?" "Playing with her feelings. She really likes your ugly ass." "I like her too. I think she fine as hell. I just don't want to hurt her. Shit I'm a senior in high school, living the single life and messing around. I'm not ready to settle down yet." "Nigga you dumb. My girl is not going to wait for you to finally confess your feelings and shit." Heaven said leaving and heading to her room. Lord sat there and thought about what Heaven said. He wondered if he could settle down with Keya. As soon as the thought came to his mind, it left when he thought about going away to college to play ball.

Chapter 24

MYA

⸺⸻◦⫸⟡⫷◦⸻⸺

Mya was enjoying living with Kyle. All he asked is that the house stay clean and she cook. The only bad thing about living with him was that he didn't allow her to talk on the phone or have company. Unfortunately, his friends were always over all times of the night. Mya was sitting on the couch doing her math homework, when Kyle walked in with a pissed look on his face. "Hey baby. What's wrong?" Mya asked looking up from her book. Kyle ignored her and headed to the kitchen. Mya didn't get to cook today because she had so much homework and she had to study for a makeup test. "Where the fuck is dinner?" Kyle yelled making Mya jump. "I didn't have time to make it yet. I was busy studying and doing homework." "So that fucking homework is more important than making sure your man is fed?" "I didn't say that Kyle. I just didn't get a chance to make it yet." Mya said looking up at him. Before Mya could get the chance to close her books, Kyle smacked them off her lap,

185

sending them flying across the room. "Now you have fucking time." Kyle said in her face. Mya was so scared she got up, but to only be met by Kyle's hand. He smacked her so hard she fell to the ground. All she was able to do was hold her face and cry. "Get your ass up and cook me some food before I hit your ass again." Mya got up off the floor, shocked he hit her. He had chocked her and grabbed her hair before, but never smacked her. Kyle sat on the couch lit up a blunt. "Shut that fucking crying up, you blowing my high." Mya knew it was going to be a mark on her face. She cooked his food and brought it to him. Mya was walking back to the kitchen when Kyle grabbed her hand. "Where are you going?" "To clean up the kitchen." Mya said in a whisper. "Naw that shit can wait. I'm horny." Kyle said unzipping his pants. Mya got on her knees and sucked his dick while he ate his food. After he bust his nut, he sent her to go clean up the kitchen and do her homework that was still all over the living room. After she finished her work, she walked in the bathroom to see her face and was ashamed. After that day, the beatings became more frequent. She would cover them up to go to school but they were getting worse that no matter how much make-up she put on, it wouldn't cover up some of them. Lord and Destiny, along with Brittany and Tamera asked her if she was okay or did she want to stay with them but she always declined. One particular day, Kyle came home from a gambling game. He lost big and was pissed off. Mya was sleep since she had school in the morning. "Mya wake up." Kyle said to her, shaking her awake. "I'm tired Kyle. I have school in a few." Mya said turning over. "I don't give a fuck. Wake the fuck up." He yelled. Mya groaned which infuriated him even more. He grabbed her by her hair and said "Bitch, I said get up." Kyle punched her in her face twice then started choking her. "I told you before about giving me attitude. Didn't I?" Kyle asked then let her go. Mya was gasping for air. Before she could even register what had happened, Kyle was pulling her night shorts down. He pushed into her so roughly that she screamed out in pain. He didn't care. He took all his frustration and anger out on her and her pussy. Mya let the tears escape her eyes while he humped away. When he finally came, he stayed inside her. "Go take a shower." Kyle said pulling out and rolling onto his back. Mya got up, but was in serious pain. She walked slowly to the bathroom to take a shower where she cried. When she got out, Kyle was sleep so she eased in the bed. With all the pain going on mentally and physically, she felt at peace when she was finally able to sleep. The next morning she didn't hear her alarm going off, but woke up to kisses on her. Mya turned around and saw Kyle. Noticing she was up, he smiled at her. "Good morning beautiful. I made you breakfast." Kyle said smiling down at her. "Good morning. Thank you." she said nervous. "I'm sorry about last night baby. I was just angry I lost a lot of money and I just lost it. I love you. Do you still love me?" Kyle asked sitting on the bed in front of her. "Yes of course I love you." Mya said looking away from him. "Good. Baby I want you to drop out of school and come work beside your man." Kyle said. "I would love to but baby I have one more year to go." Mya said. "So you want another chick to work next to me?" "No I don't." "Well I need you on my side 24/7 and you being in school ain't cutting it." Mya didn't know what to do. She knew if she said no, he would beat her again. "Ok. I'll drop out." Mya said, wanting to please Kyle. Kyle smiled at her and kissed her deeply and passionately. ... For months Mya went to every drug deal that Kyle went to. She would count his money and make sure the drugs were packed right. She was his right hand person. Ever since she started working with him his money was coming up correct, so he knew someone was stealing from him. He stopped hitting her which made her happy. She wasn't happy that she was a 15, soon to be 16 year old drop out, who couldn't talk to her friends though. Destiny had been trying to get in contact with her but Kyle would answer her phone and tell her she was busy. She even sent Scott to go check on her but Kyle would say she wasn't home. He kept her away from everyone but him. He didn't let her know her sister or brother had been trying to get in touch with her either. Mya and Kyle were sleeping well, until Mya had the urge to throw up. She jumped up and ran to the bathroom almost knocking Kyle off the bed. "Damn Mya." Kyle yelled after her. Mya was over the toilet throwing up everything she ate the night before. Getting up from the floor she looked in the mirror and saw how pale her face was. Walking back to the room, she got back in the bed only to rush back to the bathroom. "Yo, what the fuck is wrong with you?" Kyle asked looking at her with her head in the toilet. "I don't know. I can't keep nothing ..." Mya stopped and said "Shit." "Shit what?" "I might be pregnant again." Mya said nervously. "Fuck you mean you might be pregnant again?" Kyle asked. "This is how I felt the first time

I got pregnant." "Mya we can't have no fucking kid right now." "What you want me to do? I don't want to have an abortion." Kyle sighed, "I'm tripping baby. We going to raise this baby right. We need to make you a doctor's appointment." "You not upset?" Mya asked glancing at him. "Of course not." Kyle said even though he was pissed that she was pregnant. He didn't want to be a father yet but he knew not to say anything. "Can I call Destiny so she can go to the clinic with me?" Mya asked. "Yea, you can call her." Kyle said giving her permission. Mya picked her phone up calling Destiny. She was so happy she was able to talk to her. "Oh so now you know how to call someone. I was worried sick about you." Destiny said upset. "I'm sorry Dest, I will explain later. But I need you to go with me to that free women's clinic." Mya said. "That nigga gave you something?" Destiny asked, pissed. Mya rolled her eyes and said "No, but I think I might be pregnant again." "Really. Man meet me there." Destiny said already hanging up. "Ok." Mya said hanging up. She showered and got dressed. "Kyle can you drop me off?" Mya asked Kyle who was laying in the bed smoking a blunt. "Naw I got to handle some business in a little. Catch the bus. Here." Kyle said giving her money. Mya took the money and left. After catching two buses she finally made it to the clinic. She walked in and saw Destiny sitting down waiting for her. "Finally you here. I thought they were going to call your name and you weren't going to be here yet." "Well, I had to catch the bus cause my dumb boyfriend all of sudden have plans." Mya said pissed off. "He is a dickhead." "How you get here?" "Shad brought a car and Scott was with him so they picked me up. They said they are going to pick us up when we done." Before Mya could respond, they called her name. Both Destiny and Mya went to the back. After peeing in the cup, they waited. "So what are you going to do if you are pregnant?" "Have the baby." Mya said. "So tell me what's been going on with you. School is almost over and you ain't been there since... shit I can't even remember the last time you were there." "I was just not feeling school anymore. It was a waste of my time." Mya said lying. Destiny looked at her knowing she was lying. "Well how come I haven't heard from you? Lord has been driving me crazy because he hasn't heard from you, along with Laurel and Loyalty." Mya didn't know all those people were looking for her. "Wait, when did you talk to Loyalty or Laurel?" "Your sister came home to visit and was looking for you. She went to Mike's apartment then came to the neighborhood and asked what happened to his place and where you were. Loyalty been looking for you for months. I saw him the other day and asked where you were at." "I don't care." Mya said knowing she wanted to see her sister and Loyalty. Although she was pissed at them before, she missed them something terrible. "Mya you my best friend and I know you better than anyone, you do care. Laurel is worried about you." "How does she look? It's been almost two years since I saw her and Loyalty." Mya asked. "She has a mean glow about her. She looks good. Loyalty still looks fine as ever." Destiny said causing Mya to laugh. "I do miss them." Mya said looking down at her hands. Before Destiny could respond, the door opened and it was the doctor. "Ok Ms. Adams. I reviewed the urine sample. The results have concluded that you are indeed pregnant. Let's do a sonogram to see how far along you are." Mya and Destiny looked at the screen when the doctor used the wand to go over her stomach. She found out she was 2 months along. Prescribing her some prenatal pills, they left the clinic together. Destiny and Mya were looking at the sonogram picture when Shad pulled up to pick them up. "Don't tell anyone yet Destiny." Mya said. "I won't." Destiny said grabbing her hand and leading her to the car. Destiny and Scott got in the back, letting Mya sit in the front. "Hey y'all. Thank you Shad for picking us up." Mya said as she sat in the front seat. "It's no problem. Y'all hungry?" Shad asked. "I am." Destiny said. "Me too." Mya said cosigned. They drove to Buffalo Wild Wings and were seated immediately. After ordering they started to talk. "So you guys ready to graduate?" Mya asked Scott and Shad. "Hell yea." They both said. Destiny and Mya laughed at them. Shad was enjoying himself with Mya and knew why he loved her so much. He just wished she would see how much he cared about her and leave Kyle alone. In the middle of their meal, Mya's phone rang. "Hello." "Where you at?" Kyle asked. "I'm at Buffalo Wild Wings with Destiny and your brother." Mya purposely left Shad's name out because she didn't want any problems. "I told your ass to go to the doctors and back home. Yo, you must like getting your ass beat. Get the fuck home now." Kyle yelled through the phone. "Ok." Mya said before Kyle hung up on her. After that Mya lost her appetite and was ready to go. "Um Shad do you think you can take me home, now?" Mya said looking down. "Yea, let us get the check." "Mya I think you should come move in with me." Destiny said trying to reason with her best friend. She knew Kyle must have called and told her to come home. "I'm fine Destiny. I promise." They packed up their food and headed to Kyle's place. Pulling up at the building, Mya thanked them and ran in the house. Kyle was sitting on the couch smoking and drinking a beer. "Took you long enough. What the doctor said?" "I'm two months pregnant." Mya told him. Kyle just looked at her with no emotion on his face as he continued to drink his beer. "Are you happy?" Mya asked him. "I really don't give a fuck, for eal. Look we have this meeting, so I need you to dress nice. We going to the club." "Bae, I'm not old enough to get in the club." Mya said. "Mya." Kyle yelled then looked at her "Did I ask you that? I just told you to wear something to the club." "Ok." She said, not feeling like getting dressed up at all. At 10 pm, Kyle and Mya were pulling up to "Club Passion". Getting out, they walked up to the VIP section and were let in immediately. Everyone was drinking and having a good time, but Mya was sitting there feeling out of place. She was rocking back and forth to the music in her seat, while drinking cranberry juice. "Baby you want to dance?" Mya asked Kyle. "Mya don't you see me handling business right now. Just chill the fuck out." Kyle said with an attitude. Mya didn't want to be in his presence anymore so she got up. Before she could walk off, Kyle grabbed her wrist. "Where you going?" "I'm going to the bathroom." Mya said looking at him. "Hurry back cause we leaving soon." "Ok." **Loyalty...** Loyalty was chilling in his VIP section with his boys sipping on some Hen, vibing out to the music. "Nigga you good over there?" Kelly asked. "Yea I'm straight." Loyalty said drinking some more from his cup. "Aye yo Loyalty, I think that's baby sis right there." Moss said pointing towards a girl that was walking. Loyalty jumped up and looked to where Moss was pointing at. He looked at the girl and realized it was Mya. He had been looking for her ever since Mike got locked up. "I'll be back." Loyalty said not waiting for a response, just walking off. He waited by the females bathroom until Mya came out. "Long time no see." Loyalty said scaring Mya. "Shit." Mya said holding her chest, then looked at Loyalty and added "Hey big bro. Looking good." "You look good too lil sis. Where the fuck you been at? You have me and your sister worried about you." "I'm fine. After Mike got locked up, Amber took everything and left so I moved in with Kyle." "With who?" Loyalty said not hiding his anger. "Kyle my boyfriend. You know who Loyalty." She said in a duh tone of voice. "Look, you moving back home. You coming home with me and we gonna visit your sister tomorrow." Loyalty said. "I'm not moving back. I'm happy with Kyle." Mya said trying to keep her voice strong. As soon as that left her mouth Kyle appeared. "Dang baby you almost had me worried." Kyle said walking up to Loyalty and Mya. "I'm sorry. Me and Loyalty were just catching up." Mya said smiling at him. Kyle looked at Loyalty then added "You ready to go home?" "Yea, I'm ready to go." Mya said then turned her attention to Loyalty "It was good seeing you again big bro. Tell my sister I love her." "Mya just come home. I don't think you safe being with him." Loyalty said pointing to Kyle as he spoke. "Mya!" Kyle said with so much base in his voice

"Let's go." Mya looked at Loyalty one more time, then walked out the club with Kyle. Loyalty just shook his head and headed back to the VIP. "What happened with Mya?" Moss asked. "Man, that nigga got her brain washed or something. She went with him." Loyalty said shaking his head. "I just hope that nigga ain't treating her bad, because if he is I'm murdering his ass." Moss said already planning a way to take Kyle out. "Nigga who you telling." Loyalty stayed at the club for a few more hours and then decided to leave. He walked inside his condo and went straight to bed. It was 2am and he was tired. As soon as he closed his eyes, his phone rang. "What?" He answered without looking at the caller ID. "Dang, really." Laurel said. "My bad baby. I didn't look at the screen." "I was about to say." "What you doing up so late?" "I was up writing a paper and I took a break to call my future." "Look at you thinking about a nigga and shit." "Always, you know I love you so much." "I love you too... I saw Mya today?" Laurel got happy and asked back to back questions "Is she good? Does she look healthy? Where she been? Is she with you?" "Baby calm down with the questions, but yes she looks fine and healthy and no she is not with me. She has been living with Kyle." "I don't trust that nigga with my sister. I need her home." Laurel said on the verge of crying. "I know baby, but it was nothing I could do. She told me to tell you she loves you." "Loyalty I want to come home." "What you mean?" Loyalty ask sitting up in the bed. "I'm home sick. I miss you and want to wake up and go to bed to you. I miss my little sister. I miss my brother, my best friends. I even miss my parents. I just need to come back home." Laurel said crying. "Laurel this is your dream baby. I wouldn't be able to live with myself if you give up on your dream and move back here because you are homesick. Baby I miss you too. I crave your touch every night too but we gonna make it. When you walk across that Harvard stage, I will be there yelling your name." "Baby I can transfer to GW or Howard. Those are good schools also." "Babe, just sleep on it before you make any decisions." Loyalty didn't want her to give up on her dream from graduating from Harvard. "Ok. I love you." "I love you too. Now let's go to sleep. No snoring on the phone this time or I might have to hang up on you." He laughed. "I don't snore." Laurel said laughing. "If you say so."

Chapter 25

MYA...

———∘⟫⟩⟨∘⟨⟩⟨⟨∘∘———

Mya was kind of scared with the way Kyle was driving back to the house. He was speeding and she could tell he was upset but didn't want to add any fuel to his already burning flame. Pulling up to the house, Kyle got out the car, leaving Mya. After a few minutes, Mya got out the car and followed him into the house. As soon she walked over the threshold, Kyle punched her straight in the face, causing her nose to bleed. "I swear you like me beating your ass. Why the fuck was you in that nigga face for?" Kyle said hitting her again and again. Mya was in the fetal position holding her stomach and trying to protect her face. "You were planning on leaving me? Huh?" Kyle said with a kick to her stomach. "Answer me dammit." He said kicking her again in the stomach. "No Kyle I'm not going to leave you." Mya said crying. "Good, go clean yourself up." Kyle said walking out the door, leaving her on the floor crying. Mya struggled to get up but she made it and went to the bathroom. She cleaned up her bruises and took a hot shower. Making her way to the room, she climbed under the covers and went to bed. The next morning when she woke up, Kyle still wasn't home. She called him but he didn't answer. After two days of being in the house and not answering any of her friends, sister or Loyalty calls, Mya just prayed that she would find the right guidance. By the third day of no word from Kyle, her bruises were healing and she was feeling like her normal self again. She was laying on the couch taking a nap when she felt a sharp pain in her stomach. Mya went to get up but couldn't stand. The pain was too bad. She knew this pain too well. She knew she was having a miscarriage again. Picking up her phone, she dialed Kyle's number again, but got no answer. She called again and the same thing. Picking up her phone, she dialed the person she knew would be there for her. "I shouldn't even answer this phone for your ass." "Destiny it's happening again. Ugggggggggg." Mya said groaning from the pain. "What's wrong Mya? Talk to me." Destiny said worried. "Please Destiny help me. It hurts so bad." Mya said. "Scott call Shad we have to get to Mya." Mya heard Destiny tell Scott in the background. "Destiny I feel weak." Mya said feeling dizzy. She looked down and she that she had a lot of blood in her crotch area. "Mya please stay focused. We on our way." Destiny said trying to get her to keep talking. "I'm trying." Mya said feeling her eyes start to close. "Talk to me Mya. We on our way now." Destiny said frantically. Mya didn't respond. "Mya! Mya! Mya!" Destiny yelled. "Hurry Destiny." Mya said in a low, faint voice. "Hurry the fuck up Shad." Destiny said yelled. She was terrified from the idea of losing her best friend. "I'm doing damn near a 100 Destiny, what the fuck." Shad said worried about Mya as well. Shad pulled up to Mya and Kyle's building. They all took off running to the apartment. Destiny was banging on the door trying to get Mya to open it, but she was passed out on the living room floor bleeding out. Scott and Shad was about to knock the door down when they saw the maintenance man. They flagged him down and asked him to open the door, explaining the situation. He ran to the door and opened it for them. Destiny was the first person through the door and the sight that she saw caused her to fall to her knees.

To Be Continued....

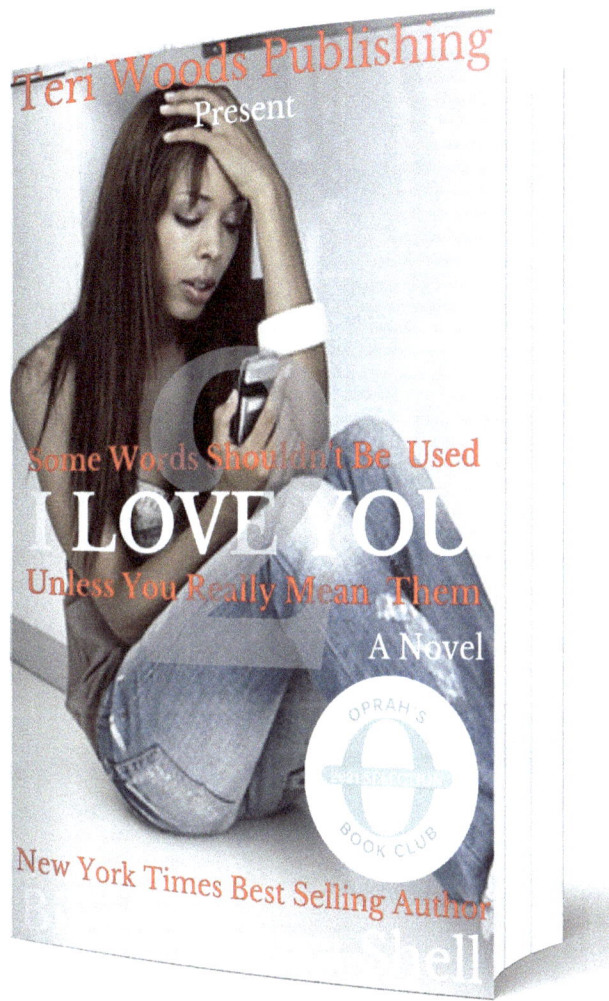

Teri Woods Publishing
Present

Some Words Shouldn't Be Used
I LOVE YOU
Unless You Really Mean Them

A Novel

New York Times Best Selling Author

SNEAK PEEK

Chapter 1

DESTINY...

⊶⊷⊷⊷⊶

As soon as Destiny saw Mya on the ground, she ran to her and held her. "Wake up Mya." Destiny cried while checking her pulse. "You still have a pulse, so you alive. Now open your eyes for me please Mya." Destiny said rocking her softly. Mya could hear her but couldn't open her eyes. She reached for her hand and gave it a squeeze, letting her know she could hear her. "She's going to be fine, but we have to get her to the doctors. She's pregnant." Destiny told Scott and Shad who both looked shocked. "Pregnant?" Shad said, almost whispering it. "Yes, now please help me carry her so we can get her to the hospital." Destiny said making a move to get up with Mya. Shad wasted no time picking Mya's limp body up off the floor, ignoring the blood leaking everywhere. All he cared about was her safety. Carefully placing her in the car, they all piled in and headed to the hospital. Shad kept Mya's head on his lap while they drove, hoping that she would be ok. As soon as they got to the hospital, Mya was rushed in the back. Destiny told the nurses she was her sister and filled out the paper work. "Where is your brother Scott?" Destiny asked pissed off. She knew that when she saw Kyle, she was going to split his shit for not being there. "I don't know baby. Do you think we should call her mother or somebody?" Scott asked sending a text to Kyle letting him know what happened and where they were at. They both moved to the waiting area and sat down. "Her mother wouldn't care. I don't want to worry Laurel but I don't have Loyalty's number either." Destiny said resting her head on Scott's shoulder. Shad was pacing back and forth, nervous for Mya. He cared about her a lot and didn't want to see her hurt. Waiting for 2 hours the doctor finally came out. "Adams family." Scott and Destiny stood up and walked to the doctor. He looked at the teens and wondered where the adult was. "Um do you all have an adult or a parent present?" The doctor asked skeptically. "We are 18 which makes us adults and that's her sister. So may you please Dr. Wells let us know how Mya is doing?" Scott said. "Ok. Well Ms. Adams had several bruises over her body that has hemorrhaged; a swollen nose and she also suffered a miscarriage. She lost a lot of blood so we did a transfusion. She will have to stay her for at least a week to be monitored. She will be ok." Dr. Wells said, then looked back at the teens and asked "Do any of you have any idea how Ms. Adams got the bruises on her body?" They all had assumptions but didn't say anything so they all said no. "Can I see her?" Destiny asked. "Sure. We moved her to the 4th floor in room 420." Dr. Wells said pointing to the elevators. They all rode the elevator up in silence, each lost in their own thoughts. When they made it to Mya's room, Destiny could barely recognize her with all the tubes coming out of her. She turned to Scott and said "I know your brother beat her." "Baby you don't know that." Scott said trying to defend his brother. "I know and if I see him I'm going to beat his ass like he did my sister." Destiny said walking over to Mya and holding her hand. The room was quiet until Destiny's phone rang. It was Tamera calling. "Hello." Destiny answered. "Where you at? We have been waiting for you and Scott." "We at the hospital. Mya's been admitted." Destiny said sadly. "WHAT! We on our way." Tamera said hanging up. After 20 minutes of being in the room and everyone in their own thoughts, Mya moved and opened her eyes. "Hey." She said weakly. "Mya you scared the shit out of me." Destiny said hugging her immediately. Mya groaned in pain causing Destiny to jump back away from her. "I'm so sorry. Did Kyle do this to you?" Mya looked at Destiny and wanted to tell her the truth. She knew that she should have, but she didn't want her judging her relationship. "No, I actually got in a fight with some girl that said she was sleeping with him three days ago." Destiny didn't believe her but she didn't want to press the issue at the moment. "Why would you fight her if you knew you were pregnant?" Shad quizzed. He knew her story wasn't adding up. Mya looked at Shad and saw the love in his eyes for her but she was still stuck on protecting Kyle. "I wasn't thinking at that moment." Mya said looking down at her hands. Shad walked over to the bed grabbed her hand and kissed it. He looked her straight in the eyes and said "Don't do anything like that again that will threaten your life." Mya looked deep in his light brown eyes and said "I won't." Just when she looked away from him, her room door opened to more people coming in, including Lord. He walked over to the bed like a big brother and asked her "What the fuck happened?" Mya explained about her "fight" with the other girl and told them she was pregnant and lost the baby. "Why the fuck were you fighting over that nigga anyway Mya? Especially pregnant." Lord said shaking his head at her. "Lord I didn't think about it." Mya said. "Yea, where is that bitch ass nigga at anyway?" Lord asked getting mad. Before anyone could reply, Kyle came in the room and looked around. He saw Lord standing on one side of Mya's bed and Shad on the other. He screwed up his face at the sight. He looked them both up and down and then looked at Mya. "Baby I'm sorry I took so long. Are you ok?" Kyle said walking up to her pushing Shad out the way. Mya looked at him with a little fear in her eyes and answered him in a weak voice, "I'm ok." "Where the fuck was you at when she was at home almost bleeding to death?" Destiny asked ready to attack him but Scott grabbed her up before she could reach him. Kyle looked at her with a death glare and said "If you must know Ms. Destiny, I was making money. I didn't have my phone on so I wasn't able to know she called but I got Scott text message once I turned my phone on." "Don't you think if you gonna fuck around on Mya, you need to keep your chicks in order?" Lord said, eyeing him angrily. "What the fuck are you talking about nigga?" Kyle asked confused. "The bitch that did this to my fucking best friend. The chick said she was fucking you and they fought." Lord said heated now. Kyle looked over to Mya. He was happy inside that she covered for him, but was pissed that her friends were in their business. Turning his attention back to Lord, he looked him up and down. "Nigga don't worry about our relationship. Bitches be out here lying. I told Mya don't be feeding into that bullshit." "Yo I should just fuck you up right now." Lord said making a step in Kyle's direction. "Mya check your boy. I already told you I don't like you around this nigga any way." Kyle said ready to meet him. "Calm down Lord please." Mya said weakly while pushing him back. "Calm down Mya? You scared of this nigga or something. Fuck that bitch ass nigga. You know what, I love you. You always gonna be my best friend and sister, but since you listening to this nigga about not being around me and shit I'll leave. Holla at me when you realize this nigga ain't shit but bad news. Get better baby girl." Lord said kissing her forehead and walking out. Shad looked over at Kyle trying to portray the supporting boyfriend and got pissed. "I'm out. Feel better Mya." Shad said looking at her then turned to Destiny and Scott "I'll wait for y'all outside." Everyone started to walk out the room leaving Scott, Destiny, Mya and Kyle. "You need me to stay with you Mya?" Destiny asked. "I'm fine Destiny. I know ma is gonna be worried about you." Mya said looking down at her hands. Times like this, she wish she could depend on her own mother. "I texted her and told her where I was. I'll be back tomorrow then." Destiny said leaning in to hug Mya's shoulder. "Ok. Love you." She said, embracing her back. "Love you too." Destiny said Scott told her to feel better and gave his brother a look of disgust as he followed Destiny out the room. Walking down the hall, Destiny looked at Scott and said "I hope you never put your hands on me." "I would never do that." Scott said pulling her into a hug as they got on the elevator. "Good, because I have uncle who will kill you after I beat your ass." Destiny said with a straight face. Scott leaned down and kissed her on the lips while laughing, causing Destiny to smile in return.

Chapter 2

LAUREL...

⟳⟫⟪⟳

After Laurel's talk with Loyalty about being home sick, she decided to finish all her assignments and finals early so she could go home for summer break. Before she left, she put all her stuff in storage and hit the road. No one knew she was coming home, not even Loyalty. She wanted to surprise him and her friends. The drive from Massachusetts wasn't bad. She planned on seeing Loyalty, then going to see her girls and track her damn sister down. Pulling up to her and Loyalty's condo, she parked in her space, grabbed her suitcase and headed to the door. When she walked in, he was on the couch sleep with only basketball shorts on. She stood and admired him, loving the view in front of her. Pulling out her phone from her purse, she snapped a picture of him. Walking up on him, she leaned down and kissed his lips softly. "I better be dreaming, because if I open my eyes and it's my homesick girlfriend, I'm going to teach her a lesson for dipping out on school." Loyalty said with his eyes still closed.

Laurel held in her laughter and hid behind the couch when Loyalty finally opened his eyes. "You might as well come out from behind the couch because I have a six sense when it comes to you." Loyalty said, stretching his arms. Laurel stood up and leaned over the couch into him. Wrapping her arms around his neck, she started to kiss on his cheek and neck. "Don't try and butter a nigga up with those soft lips of yours." Loyalty said pulling her over the couch and putting her on his lap. "I'm not buttering you up. I've just missed you a lot." "I thought we talked about you coming home next week for summer break. You better not be dipping on any classes." Loyalty said while playing with her clit through her sweat pants. "I know, but the professors let me do all my finals and assignments early so I could leave." Laurel moaned out, loving the feeling of his hand between her legs. "What your grades looking like?" Loyalty asked sucking on her neck. "They will post tomorr... mmmmm." Laurel moaned when he moved his hand inside her pants. Loyalty massaged her clit with one hand, while pulling her pants down with the other. "Good. Let's make these babies." Loyalty said stripping Laurel of all her clothes. Laurel was in heaven as her and Loyalty made love on the couch. After having multiple orgasms they both showered and got dressed. "So what you have planned today?" Loyalty asked as he tied his shoe laces. "I'm going around the way to see the girls and then go find my sister. What about you?" Laurel said pulling her boyshorts on. "I have a couple of pickups to do and then I'm going to find my wife so we can find our little sister. I'm going to take my ladies out to dinner and then you and I are going to continue making babies." Loyalty said walking over to her and kissing her on the lips. "I like that plan." Laurel said biting her lip when he pulled away. "Well let's be out." They both got in their separate cars and headed to their destinations. Laurel pulled up around her way a short time later. Since everyone was out of school already, it was packed outside. She spotted Tiara and Melanie talking on the stoop and walked up to them. "So this is what y'all do when school is over." Laurel said. They both looked at her and screamed. "Oh my gooodnesssss! We missssed your ass so much!" Tiara yelled as she stood to hug Laurel. "I missed y'all too. So what's been up?" Laurel asked sitting on the stoop with them. "Girl, since your brother got locked that nigga Cash been running round here like he the Godfather or some shit. Like he really gangsta now. Other than that, shit been mellow." Melanie said. "So, have y'all seen my mom?" Laurel asked looking up at the window of her old apartment. "Yea. We saw Ms. Liz. She looks the same and shit." Tiara said shrugging. "What about Mya?" Laurel asked anxiously. Melanie and Tiara looked at each other but didn't want to be the one to tell Laurel about her sister. "Can one of you tell me what's up with my sister?" Laurel said impatiently. She could see it on their faces that something was up. "Ok. Tamara came home a couple of days ago and told me that Mya was in the hospital. She said she got in a fight with one of Kyle chicks. She was pregnant and lost it..." Before Tiara could continue Laurel cut her off. "Hold the fuck up. You telling me that my sister is in the hospital and neither one of you ain't call and tell me." Laurel said pissed off. "I called you when I found out, but you seemed like you was on the verge of a breakdown your damn self. I couldn't put that stress on you." Tiara said trying to make Laurel see reason. Laurel knew Tiara didn't tell her to look out for her health, but she still was pissed. "What hospital?" Laurel asked. "Greater Southeast." Laurel got up and walked to the car without saying anything. When she got in, she called Loyalty. "Dang babe you just left a nigga. You miss me already?" Loyalty joked once he answered the phone. "Baby, Mya is in the hospital." Laurel said trying not to cry. "What? Which one?" Loyalty asked while turning his car in the opposite direction of where he was going. "Greater Southeast." Laurel said, holding the phone and speeding to the hospital. "I'm on my way." Loyalty said hanging up. Laurel pulled up at the hospital parking lot and got out. She ran to the front desk and got the nurses attention. "I'm looking for my sister Mya Adams." Laurel said trying to catch her breath. "She's in room 402." "Thank you." Laurel said running for the elevators and getting on. She walked to Mya's room when she reached the 4th floor and slowly pushed the door open. Her eyes zoning in on the bed, she saw that Mya was sleeping peacefully. She walked over to her bed and took a seat in the chair next to it. She grabbed Mya's hand, causing her to open her eyes. "Laurel?" Mya asked in a low voice. "It's me Mya." Laurel said smiling at her. "Oh my God. I miss you so much." Mya said smiling and then starting to cry. "I miss you too." Laurel said crying as well, pulling her into a hug. They both were hugging each other and crying. Destiny had just walked in the room when she saw them. Not wanting to interrupt their moment, she stood at the door. They finally broke their hug when they heard "I don't need no fucking pass. My sister is in that fucking room." Mya and Laurel looked at each other and said "Loyalty." "Hey y'all. Didn't want to interrupt the moment." Destiny said once they looked at her standing by the door. "Looking good little sis." Laurel said to Destiny as she walked over to them. "Looking good yourself big sis." Destiny said giving Laurel a hug then passing Mya the food she went and got her. Loyalty finally came in the room with Moss and Kelly behind him. "Yo, fucking rent-a-cops blow the shit out of me." Loyalty said Mya smiled when she saw all of the people she considered family in the room. "Damn sis. You needed a break from that nigga that bad that you had to come to the hospital?" Moss said causing everyone to laugh. "Shut up Moss." Mya said laughing. "On the real. What happened to you?" Loyalty asked when the laughter died down. "Um." Mya began. She always felt like she couldn't lie to Laurel and Loyalty. They always knew if she was being truthful. "Ummm what? We waiting." Loyalty said. "Some girl came to me and said she was sleeping with Kyle. We got into a fight and I was pregnant. She kicked me in my stomach and made me have a miscarriage." Mya said not making eye contact with them. "Again Mya. Stop fighting over that piece of shit nigga. What he had to say about it? Matter of fact, where he is?" Laurel asked, waving her arm around the room. "He had some business to handle. He told me to stop believing these girls out here." Mya said still not making eye contact. Loyalty didn't say anything. He just looked at Mya knew she was lying. Before anyone else could say anything the doctor walked in.

"Hello Ms. Adams. I see you have a full house today." Dr. King said, taking in the new faces in the room. "Yea Dr. King. That's my older sister Laurel and my brother in law." Mya said pointing to Laurel and Loyalty. Dr. King shook Loyalty and Laurel hands and then moved to check Mya's vitals. "Everything is looking good Ms. Adams." "Thank you." Mya said. Loyalty and Laurel followed Dr. King out of the room. "Hey doc can we talk to you for a second." Loyalty said walking up to the doctor as he turned around. "Sure, what can I do for you all?" "What really happened to my little sister?" Loyalty asked. He was going to find out the truth, one way or another. "Well when she came in through the emergency room, she had several bruises over her body and she lost a lot of blood due to the miscarriage. She had to have a transfusion. Upon her coming to, we asked where the bruising came from and she said she was in a fight." The doctor explained. "So how long will she be in here?" Laurel asked. "Well when your other sister filled the paperwork out, she didn't put any insurance. She is actually doing better, so we might have to discharge her in the next two days. We really need her to stay longer to monitor her blood pressure though. She also had swelling around her brain which was another concern for us." "Don't worry about the cost. I will pay the bill. Just make sure my sister is perfect before she leaves." Loyalty said. "Well do sir." The doctor said shaking Loyalty's hand. Laurel and Loyalty spent the whole day with Mya after their talk with her doctor. In the back of their minds, they knew Kyle was responsible for Mya being in the hospital. It was only a matter of time before they got their hands on him. —*—*— Mya... Mya woke up and looked around at her empty room. Laurel and Loyalty spent the whole day with her and she could honestly say she missed them so much. She looked to the night stand and saw a note in her sister's hand writing. Mya, You fell asleep on us so we went home to get some rest. I will be back in the morning to see you with your favorite breakfast: French toast and bacon. Oh and when you get discharged, you coming and living with us. No, if, ands or buts. Love you sis Laurel Mya just laughed at the note. She knew her sister was serious about her living with them. "What got you smiling so hard?" Kyle said walking in the room. "Oh, just a note my sister wrote me. She is home for summer break and came to see me." Mya said. "Oh." Kyle said not liking the idea of her and her sister back in contact. He knew if Laurel was around again, she would stop Mya from seeing him. "So, how everything been?" Mya asked changing the subject. "Busy, but my money not coming up right like when I got you on my side." Kyle said kissing her cheek. Mya smiled and said "I will be back on your arm in no time." "That's what I need to hear." Kyle said smirking. He knew he had Mya where he wanted her. "My sister wants me to move with her when I get out the hospital." Mya told him, looking down at her hands. Kyle screwed his face up and looked at her. "Is this your way to tell me you leaving me or something?" "No, I was just letting you know." Mya said starting to get nervous. "Are you going with her?" Kyle asked, moving closer to her bed. Mya looked at him and saw the fear of losing her in his eyes. "No, I'm staying with you." Mya said, trying to please him. Kyle smiled down at her. He leaned over and kissed her passionately on the lips. "I love you Mya." Kyle said looking in her eyes. "I love you too Kyle." "Let's leave here now. I hate hospitals." Kyle said pulling her sheets back. "I'm not sure if I can leave now." Mya said looking up at him. "I'm going to go get the doctor and if they say you good to go, are we leaving?" Kyle asked already knowing the answer. "Yes." Mya said reluctantly. Kyle went and got the doctor. He came back shortly after and checked Mya out. Although he recommended bed rest and some prescriptions, he discharged her. The car ride home was quiet until Mya realized they were going in the wrong direction to their house. "Kyle where are we going? We live the other way." Mya said looking at the scenery around her. "It's a surprise baby." Kyle said holding her hand. They pulled up to a nice house and Kyle pulled in the drive way. They both got out and stood in front of the mini mansion. "Welcome home baby." Mya smiled and remembered when she was younger and her family lived in a house like the one she was looking at before her father went to prison. "I love it." she said jumping in Kyle's arms and kissing him. Laurel... Laurel got off the elevator with food for Mya in her hand. When she pushed opened her door, she saw that the bed was empty as well as the room. Laurel went to the nurse's station to get information on her sister's whereabouts. "Excuse me." Laurel said looking at the nurse on duty. "Yes. How may I assist you?" "Do you know if they moved Mya Adams to another room?" The nurse looked her name up and said "Actually Ms. Adams was discharged this morning." "What? Who signed? She is only 16." Laurel was on the verge of becoming hysterical.

"It says Kyle Johnson signed her out." The nurse said. Laurel wanted to cry but she held it in and said "Thank you." When she left the hospital, got in her car and called Mya's phone. "The number you are trying to reach has been disconnected." Laurel hung up the phone and headed home. Loyalty was on the phone when Laurel walked in crying. "My nig, I have to hit you back. Wifey is home." Loyalty said ending his call and walking Laurel. "What's wrong?" he asked while pulling her into his arms. "She was gone. He discharged her and her phone is off." Laurel said crying harder. "I just want my family back, Loyalty. I miss them." Loyalty held her while she cried. He was going to make it his goal to make Laurel's wish come true. All he wanted was for his future wife to be happy. Getting her family back was going to do it. He was willing to do what he had to do no matter how long it would take.

Chapter 3

(2 YEARS LATE)

⊷⊷≫〰⊛〰≪⊶⊶

Two years had passed and so much had changed. After Laurel left the hospital and cried on Loyalty's shoulder, she woke up the next day and decided she wanted to finish college early. She wanted to marry Loyalty and move on with their lives. Deciding to go to summer school, she finished her undergraduate studies a year early and was now in her first year of law school at Harvard. Loyalty would visit her all the time when she didn't fly home. He was still in the process of getting her family back together again. He hired the top lawyers to work on her father's and brother's case. He was even paying Liz visits to get to know her better. The only hard thing was finding Mya. Kyle really had a hold on her. He had been trying to find out where she lived now, with no such luck. Destiny and the girls had graduated from high school without Mya, even though it was weird to not have all four of them together to walk across the stage, they managed. Destiny was determined to leave DC and no one was stopping her. She was accepted and going to Spelman in Atlanta while Scott was going to attend Le Cordon Bleu College of Culinary Arts Atlanta. Even with the distance and strain on Mya's and Destiny's friendship, she was always thinking about Mya. Destiny would get a call out of the blue from Mya from time to time to let them know she was doing ok, since she didn't have a way to get in contact with her unless she called. She would always tell her to come stay with her, but she would always decline the offer. Shad still thought about Mya all the time but was now a sophomore at Johnson C. Smith University studying business. He didn't take a year off like his boys since he didn't have a girl to wait for. He just wanted to leave DC and start fresh. He was no longer Lil Shad, now he was a ladies man that every girl wanted, but the only girl he wanted to be his forever was in his past. Only thing he knew was that she still and forever have his heart. Mya and Kyle's relationship was still the same. He stopped beating her for a little then it started back. Now Mya cope's with the pain by drinking

Chapter 4

MYA...

⟫⟩⟩⟩⟩⟨⟨⟨⟨

Mya walked in the house from getting her hair done since Kyle told her they were going out that night. "Where you been at?" Kyle asked. "I went to go get my hair done. You said we going out tonight." Mya said alarmed. "Didn't I tell you to call me when you leave this fucking house?" Kyle said coming towards her. Mya's back was up against the door as Kyle stood over her. "I did call you but you didn't answer." "Don't that mean stay your dumb ass in the house Mya?" Kyle questioned. Mya didn't say anything. "Bitch I know you hear me talking to you." He said, pushing her shoulder. Keeping her head lowered, she replied, "Yes." Next thing Mya knew, she tasted copper. Kyle had smacked her so hard across the face, blood insistently came from her mouth. He didn't stop with smacking her. He punched and kicked her over and over. All Mya could do was take the beating she was receiving. Once Kyle got tired he looked down at her. "You make me do this shit to you. Now your ass has to stay in the house." Kyle said walking out the door, leaving her on the floor beaten and bloody. Mya pulled herself off the floor and slowly walked to bathroom. She looked in the mirror and was disappointed by what she saw. The person looking back at her was no longer the feisty, beautiful, confident Mya Adams. This girl looking at her was a battered, scared, unloved woman. Mya used to have curves, skin that glows and sparkling eyes that were full of life. Now she was thin, with dark dull eyes, and paleness to her skin. "Who are you?" Mya asked herself while staring in the mirror. Cleaning herself up, she went to her room and looked at the pictures she hid from Kyle. It was a picture of her and her family, and another one of her and her friends that she missed so much. She picked up her phone and dialed Destiny's number. "Hello." Destiny answered on the 3rd ring. "Hey Destiny." Mya said hearing a lot of noise in her background. "Is this my sister from another mister?" Destiny asked causing Mya to laugh. "Of course it is. Is this a bad time?" "It's my going away party. I'm still lost as to why you not here." "I totally forgot Des, I'm so sorry. I wanted to call and tell you I love you and live it up in ATL." Mya said sadly. Mya didn't forget about the party. She wanted to be there but Kyle told her if she stepped foot back in her old neighborhood, he would kill her. "It's ok. I love you too and I will. Maybe you will come and visit me." Destiny said hopefully. "I plan on it. Have fun. I will call you when I can." "Ok." Destiny said even though she didn't want to hang up. She knew Mya was in danger and every time she tried to help her she don't want the help. She kept saying everything was ok. Mya hung up with Destiny. Looking at the photo of her and her family, she stared at them smiling. Phone in hand, she dialed Laurel's number but blocked her number from being seen. While the phone was ringing, she was having second thoughts. She started to hang up when the other line picked up. "Hello." Laurel said skeptically. Mya didn't know what to say, so she kept quiet on her end. It's been two years since she talked to her sister and she was scared that she would be mad at her. "Hello." Laurel said again impatiently. "I'm sorry Laurel." Mya cried into the phone. "I love you." "Mya?" Laurel said on the verge of tears. "It's me." "I've been worried about you. Are you ok?" Laurel asked. She desperately wanted to see her. "I'm sorry for making you worry. I'm ok." Mya said. She knew Kyle was home when she heard a car pull into the drive-way. "Laurel I love you. I will call you another time. I have to go." Mya said hanging up. Kyle walked in the house and went to their room. When he walked in, he saw Mya on the bed with an ice pack on her cheek. "Look, I'm sorry for doing that to you. Do you still love me?" Kyle asked handing her a small opened box. In it was a shining gold diamond necklace. "Yes I still love you." Mya said carefully taking the box from his hands. Mya was so used to this routine. He beat her, make her clean herself up, come home with a gift, ask do she still love him, she say yes, they have make up sex. When she started to heal some, he would end up doing the shit all over again. "That's my girl." Kyle said kissing her while pushing her back on the bed. Mya was so tired of this relationship but didn't know how to get out. The sex was the same every time too. He would be rough with her, cum and then make her shower. As expected, after the

15 minutes of Kyle pounding her, he came in her and then told her to get in the shower. Mya walked out the shower in a towel and saw Kyle fully dressed to head to the club. She already knew she wasn't going out the house with her face looking the way it did. "Look Mya I'm going to the club. I'll see you later." Kyle said kissing her forehead and leaving out. "Ok, be safe." Mya said, happy to be rid of him for the time being. As soon as the door closed and Mya was alone, she went to her best friend: the vodka bottle. As she drunk the vodka, she became numb and dreamed she was in a better, happier place.

ABOUT
THE AUTHOR

New York Times & International Best Selling Author
Billie Dureyea Shell was born in Compton California and
now lives in Ladera Heights with his wife and
kids who he loves to spend time with.
He is the Owner of several properties in the Los Angeles
area and gives back to his community by providing low
income housing to those who need it.
He stated "It doesn't matter where you at or where you
from it's what you do with your time. There's nothing you
can't do if you put your mind to it".

www.ingramcontent.com/pod-product-compliance
Lightning Source LLC
Chambersburg PA
CBHW070531100726
47907CB00004B/1074